Backyard Horse Tales 2

Frosty
and the
Nightstalker

Jackie Anton

First published by Dog Ear Publishing
4010 W. 86th Street, Ste H
Indianapolis, IN 46268
www.dogearpublishing.net

dog ear PUBLISHING

ISBN: 978-1-4575-175180

This book is printed on acid-free paper.

This book is a work of fiction. Places, events, and situations in this book are purely fictional and any resemblance to actual persons, living or dead, is coincidental.

Printed in the United States of America

Acknowledgements

Thanks to both of my daughters, Patricia and Kellie for endless hours spent helping me develop this story line, as well as proofreading and initial copyediting.

Sandy Shipley in addition to the fantastic cover art and illustrations read each draft and collaborated with me each step of the way on this tale. Thank you so much, Sandy.

I would be remiss not to thank my editor, Cliff Carle, who helped me pull Frosty's tale together. Cliff also edited my award winning "Backyard Horse Tales: Sox 2nd Edition,"

E-book format and submission, on Smashword.com and Amazon.com, is the work of Jody Kihara.

This book is penned in memory of my first love,
Royal Bees Frosty Britches,
who inspired this story.
Frosty's tale is also dedicated to all of our
Appaloosa friends, past, present, and future.

TABLE OF CONTENTS

Typical Appaloosa Coat Patterns

Blanket-Any color with white over hips with spots

Blanket-Any color with white over hips no spots

Leopard-White with any color spots

Any color with white snowflake spots

Blue or Red Roan with Varnish Marks

Any color with white spots over hips

Travois....A method of transporting loads of tepees, household goods, food and people.

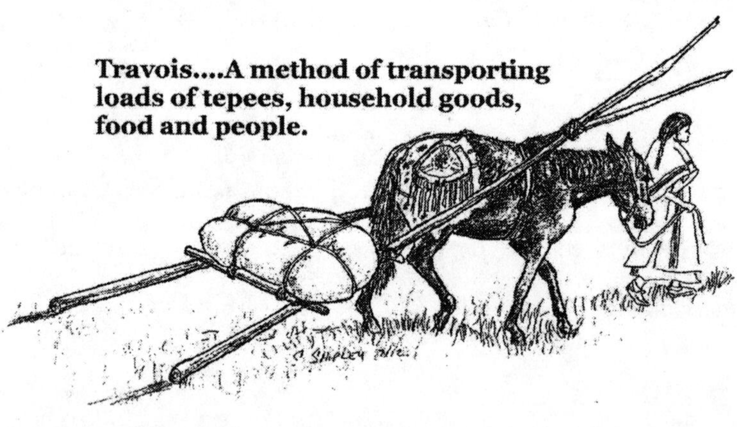

1

May, 1968 Hi-Lo Farms

My head felt heavy and everything went fuzzy. Life isn't easy for a horse. We have to put up with a lot of horse pucky from humans, and deal with strange experiences that don't make sense to us! For instance, the vet had just given me a shot. Weird! My annual spring shots never made my head spin, or affected my vision. I fought to remain standing by bracing my legs so that I wouldn't fall over. He administered another shot, and one that did me in. I was unable to resist the pull of gravity any longer, and sunk to my knees in the front paddock of Hi-Lo Farms boarding stable.

I awoke stretched out in the sun and had totally lost track of time. The ground beneath me was much colder than when I had gone to sleep; my disconnect from the world could have been minutes, hours, or days for all I knew. I gazed around as I struggled to stand, but my legs where wobbly like those of a newborn foal. At first I thought that my confusion and weak legs were a result of the double whammy of shots that had made me black out. After I planted my hooves in a wide stance so that I wouldn't topple over again, panic seized my insides. I didn't have a clue where I was! This sure wasn't the boarding stable in Ohio that had been my home for the past year! I desperately tried to focus my blurry eyes. My terror grew, and threatened to overwhelm me. I was in a strange alien world with no point of reference.

I'm standing high on a hill overlooking a crystal clear river. Once more I blink in an attempt to clear my vision. On the opposite bank graze a large herd of horses. Most of them have spotted coats that are as familiar to me as my mother and the rest of my family on the farm where I was born. Behind the grazing strangers I see great snowcapped mountains! Did the vet give me too much tranquilizer? Am I dead, and is this horse heaven? I'm frightened out of my young mind. "I want to go home to Marcie." I whinny, "but I don't know how to get there."

The lush valley and purple mountains with their snowy peaks faded along with the large band of horses as the drugs worked out of my system. I had returned home to my paddock in the place the humans called *Olmsted Falls*. Marcie was sitting on the ground next to me; joy flooded through me at the sound of her voice. She continued to talk to me softly and stroked my neck until I was awake enough to roll up to a sitting position. She stood up, and gave a tug on my lead. My human encouraged me to stand.

"*Come on, Frosty, on your feet. You've been down way too long, and scared the wits out of me. The veterinarian said gelding a two-year-old would be an easy procedure. Up! Come on,*" and then she made a loud smooching sound like when she chased me around when we played in the round pen.

I pushed with my back legs and staggered to a standing position, but I had a little trouble walking straight. Someone kept tilting the earth beneath my hooves! I nuzzled Marcie seeking comfort and reassurance. She stayed by my side until I was able to walk better, and began to act more like myself again. Sweet and tender shoots of grass caught my attention as I browsed from the confines of my lead searching for the yummiest morsels.

Marcie must have been satisfied that I was no longer under the influence of the powerful tranquilizer because she unhooked the snap of the rope lead and turned me loose. She stayed with me a while longer as I roamed the paddock looking for patches of clover. I avoided the spot where I had just been changed from a stallion to what Marcie had called a *gelding*. The bottom line was that the procedure almost cost me my life!

It was gone—the dream, the drug induced hallucination, the vision—whatever it was. The entire experience had been forgotten as I continued to search for the tasty clover hidden in the pasture grass. Little did I know then that these visions or trips to another time would haunt me for a huge hunk of my life.

A couple of hours later, I had my fill of clover appetizer. I was very thirsty, and ready for my dinner. The tantalizing sounds of buckets being emptied then refilled with fresh water, and the rattle of the oat bin tickled my ears. Horses already in their stalls were nickering, "Feed me first!" My tummy as well as my ears told me it was time to eat.

"Marcie, where are you?" I whinnied.

She materialized from the opening in the large double doors of the barn. The same one echoing with all the mouthwatering sounds that always accompanied feeding time. I smacked my lips and swallowed, practically drooling, while waiting for her to reach the paddock gate to lead me back to my stall.

It would be several more days before I stopped fretting whenever Marcie was out of my sight and I was once more able to get a good night of sleep. I guess, looking back on it, I'd been afraid she would disappear, or that I would fall asleep and wake up in that strange otherly world with out her. I often felt that strange shadows from the distant past lurked in the dark of night just waiting for me to let my guard down. I spent much of those sleepless nights recalling how Marcie and I'd become partners a little more than a year ago.

Hinckley breeding farm 1967

The first time I'd laid eyes on Marcie I was a yearling. It was about two months after my first birthday that fell on the last day of the month the humans call March. Until that time I was a happy and carefree kid, romping around the farm with the other colts. I had not been upset at weaning time like most of the other foals. My mom, Haysetta, had prepared me for what is usually a traumatic event.

"I'm going to have another foal next spring, Frosty, and it's time for you to join the rest of the herd. It is just the way of things, son." She made weaning sound so natural I didn't even question her.

Mom 's coat was a bright white with a few tiny spots scattered here and there. I looked like a small dark shadow glued to her side or following behind for the first month of my life. The next five months I grew stronger, running and engaging in mock battles with the other colts. I was eating grass, some hay, and the sweet molasses flavored grain. Mom gradually pushed me away from her delicious milk supply. I nursed less and less. Thanks to Mom's kind manner, I had zero problems when we were taken away from our mothers. Some of the other colts and fillies were really upset, and so were their mothers. My little sister was born the day before my first birthday. She was real cute, and looked just like a small version of our mother. It was fun to watch her frolic at Mom's side like I used to.

A small human, with a long dark brown mane and grass colored eyes, had come to our farm to look at an older horse. She wore a ball cap with a tail of hair sticking out the back opening. It was cool that day, and she wore a puffy red vest. She wasn't very tall. Her legs only reached halfway down the sides of Lark. All the humans on our farm were tall with white hair, and there was something different about her. She fascinated me, so I stalked them as she rode the Palomino mare around. Lark seemed to like her small rider. She wasn't tossing her head in the air, like usual, and her ears were perked forward instead of plastered back displaying her nasty temper. Their test ride had taken them around the outside perimeter of the fenced pasture that enclosed me and the rest of the herd. I felt her gaze on me as I tracked them. I whinnied a hello, snorted, and pranced around showing off for her. She laughed at my antics, which encouraged me even more.

She came back the next day, minus the dark blue chaps that had covered her jeans, she was dressed much the same as when I'd first seen her. She walked me around, brushed me, and checked my feet. I was on my best behavior. Her mom had tried to talk her out of buying me.

"Marcie, it will be a whole year before you can even start to ride him. You would be better off with the older mare. Young stallions can be a handful even for the most experienced horsemen."

"I know, Mom, but there is something special about this colt. He's very calm, his eyes are so kind and wise for a yearling. He's the one I want."

She reminded her mom that she was twenty-two now, working, and could afford to keep me for the time I required to mature. It was a huge

relief to me that she held her ground; I'd felt this instant connection between us like we were meant to be together. After I overheard their conversation, I knew that she'd felt it too.

My new home, Hi-Lo Farms, was only a short trailer ride from Hinckley, Ohio where I had been born. I would live at Hi-Lo for the next three years. I learned a lot that first year with Marcie. Often her body language made it obvious to me when I'd messed up, or pushed her good nature a little too far.

Marcie and I went to a few Appaloosa shows. She was proud of me and always praised my performance when I stood up and did all the maneuvers required of me, even when the other stallions in the halter class were acting up. "*Good job, Frosty.*"

It wasn't until, Lorry, one of the snooty high stepping Saddlebred mares, who also had lived at Hi-Lo, inquired about the color of my ribbons that I began to understand their significance.

Lorry snickered nastily with a superior attitude and looked down her long narrow nose at me. "Well, little bumpkin, word has it that you went to an App-a-loser show. Did you place? If so what color of ribbon did you come home with?"

"Marcie and I came home with two ribbons," I boasted.

She let out a loud whinny and shook her head. "I asked what color they were, you backwoods dunce."

It takes a lot to get me riled, but she was pushing my limits. Just what makes her think that she's smarter than me? I tried to be a gentleman and hold my temper. "The ribbon we got on Saturday was yellow, and Sunday we collected a red ribbon before we headed for home."

"Well, you can forget about the yellow one. My human, Thurston, says, '*Anything that isn't first or second place—blue or red—is an embarrassment and belongs in the trash*'."

That did it! I had turned, lifted my tail, and farted right in her stuck-up face.

Lorry and her equally self-important owner with the funny name moved away a few months later. They went to a fancy, high priced, training facility. I'm not just speaking for myself when I say she wasn't missed by any of us at Hi-Lo. Yes, she was gone, but her taunts about the color of my ribbons played in my head at the next few shows.

Up until my two-year-old spring when I became a gelding, I had always been shown in the stallion halter class. I would stand with my legs squared up like Marcie and I had practiced for hours on end. My polished hooves never moved while we waited in the lineup for our turn to walk up to the judge, then I squared up again so that he or she could walk around me checking out my conformation—that is how well they thought I was put together. When the judge was finished checking out my muscular body, I trotted off in a straight line, and showed off my well-formed legs as they tracked straight and true.

I think it's fair to say that most judges liked me. At that time, I consistently placed in the top three, and my halter class usually numbered at least twenty horses. Marcie would console me with, "*Judges feel obligated to place a loud colored horse first for the yearling stallion class.*"

I believe Marcie was correct about that. Most of the horses who received their ribbons before me had leopard coat patterns; others that placed above me sported huge white blankets loaded with spots. At that time in my life I was a dark chocolate color with black spots under my dark coat and just a little sprinkle of white hairs on my rump that looked a little like sugar or frosting.

Marcie said, *"That's the reason your first owners named you 'Frosty Britches'."*

That's what they called me at the shows when they announced the names of the horses awarded ribbons; my friends simply called me *Frosty*. My mother told me when I was little, "son, you are the only dark colored foal ever born to me, and I have foaled more than a dozen before you. The star decorating the middle of your forehead, and the small white sock on your left hind foot contrast beautifully with your dark coat."

Like many Appaloosas, I had pink skin with black spots that was really hard to miss. My *parti-colored* skin contrasted big time with my dark coat too; the colorful skin covered my nose, circled my eyes, and my private parts. White sclera ringed my dark brown eyes, giving me an almost human look, and my hooves were vertically striped; all of these traits are common among what humans call *the Appaloosa horse.*

Marcie and I went to a few shows where I showed in the two-year-old gelding class. To my surprise, many of the same horses who had been in the previous years stallion class with me were now in my gelding class too. I was stalled between two of my half brothers at the second show that Marcie took me to as a gelding. I questioned them about their gelding experiences.

Chel-C proudly informed me, "I didn't have any trouble when I was gelded and was down only a short time."

Sailor though admitted, "Just like you, Frosty, I required a second shot."

My interest was piqued. "Were you down a long time, Sailor?"

"I'm not sure, Frosty. My vet and the other humans were worried about me, so I guess that I was down longer than was usual. It took me a good twenty minutes to stand once I woke up. Then, I staggered around for a while before I could walk normally again."

I had to ask. "Did you have any strange dreams or visions while you were asleep?"

"Not that I recall. Why did you?"

I didn't want to be seen as an oddball. "Uh…no, but I've heard from older horses that crazy dreams or strange visions can come from too much tranquilizer."

Sailor and Chel-C both looked at me askance and I knew they could tell I was covering something up. Fortunately, they didn't call me on it. Thinking back, the whole experience was a vague memory, but just enough remained to make me wonder if someone—anyone else—had gone through anything like that. I only asked a couple of other new geldings, and when none of them had experienced anything remotely similar, I began to worry why it had only happened to me.

Most of the residents of Hi-Lo were American Saddlebreds like the recently departed Lorry. Sprinkled among the high steppers were a couple of Arabian mares, a Pinto pony, a black Tennessee Walker gelding, and yours truly.

Lorry's old stall became home for Spy. He turned out to be a really neat guy. Spy told the rest of us, "I'm only one half Saddlebred. Surely you've noticed my black and white Pinto markings?"

Spy was a parade horse. When we shared a paddock, I loved to hear his stories of traveling down paved roads with crowds of people lining both sides of the parade route. How awesome!

Marcie and I spent two and a half years at Hi-Lo. As a yearling I learned to work on a lunge line and to drive with the homemade driving lines that Marcie had woven from baling twine attached to the ring on either side of my halter.

I learned to stand with my lead line dangling on the ground, and later when my bridle reins dropped that was my cue to stand where I was and wait for Marcie.

I heard her tell Ken, the owner of Hi-Lo, *"My Frosty is really getting the hang of how to ground tie."*

I'd also mastered the commands to walk, trot, canter, whoa, and back before the first saddle ever hit my back. One day I overheard Marcie talking to Ken while she helped him fill our water buckets.

"Frosty is so smart. He grasps every new lesson quickly and never forgets anything."

"You know, Marcie," Ken nodded, *"I think Frosty is an old soul in a young body. He already knows a lot more than most of us. That could be the reason for his tractability and ease of training."*

I didn't know exactly what the old gray haired trainer was talking about, and I wondered if Marcie did, but she didn't comment on Ken's assessment of me. The bottom line was that I just loved Marcie. I enjoyed our workouts and time together, and I could tell the feelings were mutual.

To the humans at the barn, who worked with or owned the other horses, I was an oddity. It was commonplace for me to have faces stare at me through the bars of my stall; their mouths hung open like they were trying to catch flies! Often our workouts would be interrupted, while Marcie answered questions like, *"What's with the peculiar markings on your horse?"* The other horses' owners would often bring their friends to see the Appaloosa.

As a breed we were just beginning to emerge in that area of Ohio. People were very curious about me. It was a good thing that I did not mind being touched, or having folks gawk at me; in fact, I was rather proud of my *"weird looking rear end."*

1969

The following spring I had all but forgotten my strange vision of the prior year. Shed of our long winter coats, we horses basked in the warm sun that reflected off our sleek bodies. That was the time of year horse shows were in full bloom. We only traveled to four shows the year I turned three. Shows were nothing new to me; I'd been showing at halter since I was only four months of age, and still at my mother's side. However, showing with Marcie on my back, instead of at the end of my lead, was a whole new experience. It didn't take me long to figure out what was expected of me, and I placed at most of the open shows. "Open" meaning any breed of horse or pony could compete.

Marcie and I would travel to the open shows with our Arabian, Half Arab, or Saddlebred friends, hitching a ride in their horse trailers. When we attended the Appaloosa shows we went with the owners of the farm where I was born.

Open shows were a royal pain in my spotted butt! Curious exhibitors and spectators alike would ask Marcie, "*What kind of horse is that?*

She'd answer, "*Frosty is an Appaloosa.*"

You'd think that we could get back to our pre-class warm up. Wrong! The follow up questions would start, "*What's an Appaloosa? And where on earth did you find him?*" Marcie was friendly and fielded the questions thrown at her with grace.

Only once do I recall being tempted to step on some guy's toes; this loudmouth kept insisting that I was a mule! He argued, "*Only mules got dark bodies and pale colored muzzles.*" He wouldn't back off, and his obnoxious attitude pushed Marcie to the brink.

"*Mister, if you can find a mule as nice looking and as obedient as my horse I will buy him.*" Then she turned me around and we walked away. After that encounter I began to look forward to the long trailer rides across the state to Appaloosa shows; where I was just one of many horses who sported mottled skin, the wide eyed look inherent with white sclera, and vertical striping on our polished hooves.

With out a doubt the highlight of my three-year-old summer had been my introduction to the trails of what Marcie called "*The Cleveland Metro Parks.*" One sunny afternoon, I disembarked from a four-horse trailer along with several of my stable-mates. I gazed around, somewhat concerned, as I backed out and stepped to the ground. Our human companions had brought us to the middle of nowhere! In reality, it was a remote parking area in a section of the park our humans called *Rocky River Reservation*.

That was my first experience on the trails of what was also know as *The Emerald Necklace*. I know that bit of information because I heard Marcie explaining the park system to Carol, Raffella's owner, who was new to Ohio. Raffella was the Half Arab in the trio of mares accompanying me on my first ride. She and her Arabian mother were red chestnuts with flaxen manes and tails, wide blazes and four white stockings. They looked more like twins than mother and daughter. Carol's mother Ann rode the full Arab, Jazz. Our other trail companion, Pat, was riding a plane bay Saddlebred with no white markings. The mare's name was Amy, and she was an old hand at this trail riding stuff. I listened to Marcie as she told Carol more about the parks.

"Cleveland is the largest city in Cuyahoga County. Its northern border is Lake Erie. The other borders of the county are decorated with a network of parks and trails that form a kind of necklace."

Amy towered over the rest of us as we left the parking area and entered the horse trail. Jazz and Raffella were a bit shorter than me, and Marcie said that I was fifteen hands and two inches, or sixty-two inches tall. You can do the math. It is a bit beyond me, but I filed away the human explanation: *When measuring a horse from the ground to the point of the withers, four inches equals one hand.*

Strange shadows cropped up quite unexpectedly as the sun played tricks shining through the thick foliage that formed a canopy above our heads. An occasional rabbit hopped out from the underbrush, or a deer would dart across the trail in front of us. "More please?" I was eating up the experience.

"Be careful what you wish for, Frosty." Amy cautioned. "This is a short ride, and an easy trail to negotiate. Future trail rides will get longer and more difficult as you get older and gain experience."

Amy had tried to temper my exuberance. Her words would occasionally play back in my mind on subsequent rides.

Not much bothered me, but a few rides later my first river crossing undid me somewhat. Swift water flowed before me, and I watched with apprehension as my companions stepped into the current. It was difficult for me to judge the depth of what was before me, and I paid close attention while the more experienced mares casually proceeded to cross. Water swirled around their legs, and though the depth had only reached their knees I held my breath expecting them to be swept away.

"Come on Frosty, Get your hooves wet." I heard Jazz tease me.

I stepped into the river at Marcie's urging with much reluctance and a queasy feeling in my tummy. I quickly discovered why that body of water was named Rocky River. A few steps from the gradual embankment, my shod hooves came in contact with slippery rocks and large slabs of slimy shale. Each step caused me to slip on the tricky footing that was hidden beneath the bubbling foam of the fast flowing surface. At one point I just froze. Then, I heard Amy whinny.

"Come on, big guy, you can do it. You're so brave and level headed most of the time. Are you going to let this little puddle throw you?"

I whinnied back to her, "You call this a puddle?"

The three mares and their riders were safely on the other side waiting for Marcie and me. With Marcie's gentle urging and the older horses' encouragement, I tried again. After all, if the two smaller mares could cross, so could I. ...Right? ...It was a good thing I was born with a dark coat, and the mares couldn't see me blushing at all the fuss they made when I finally climbed up the opposite bank to join them.

More river crossings were added on later trail rides, and we usually returned to the horse trailers the same way we had started out. On these rides each river crossing was traversed from both directions. On my first few trail rides the crossings descended on a gradual slope, and the rise on the opposite bank was just as gradual. My confidence grew, and I became more accomplished at navigating the river crossings. You guessed it, Marcie took me on more challenging trails. That is when the crossings became more difficult: steep banks slick with mud or loose shale, and deeper, faster water. Unbidden images of deep, fast flowing, cold water stirred in the back of my mind, and I imagined myself losing my balance, slipping into the current and drowning.

Only my trust in Marcie and my desire to please her provided me with the motivation to tackle those tricky approaches. Well...that, and not wanting to look like a wimp in front of my trail companions who still crossed before I did and thought nothing of swimming the deeper waters. I kept to myself the fact that if given my choice I would never go near a river.

Early that fall, Marcie and a few friends from Hi-Lo held a picnic along with our trail ride. After a short morning ride, the five of us horses were tied back at the trailer to munch on the alfalfa-timothy grass stuffed in our hay-bags. If I'd known what was coming, I may not have been so impatient with the picnic delay.

"Spy, will you look at our humans, playing with those long thin sticks with the big round loops on the end and smacking that small feathered object back and forth. I think they forgot all about us."

"That's fine with me, Frosty. I'm just as happy standing here in the shade enjoying my hay."

In addition to the three mares who usually accompanied me on these rides, two other geldings were in our trail group. Spy and his owner Sandy joined us, as did Midnight, the black Tennessee Walker and his owner Chris. It was really nice to have a couple of guys on the ride for a change.

We were, finally, on the trail again. I noticed that the current was unusually calm at the first few river crossings. Even the water level was lower than usual. I climbed down a very steep bank and was fully focused on my footing. It had escaped my attention that there was not an exit on the opposite side. Instead, there was a steep cliff rising where there should have been a way out. I was extremely nervous walking in the middle of the river. I felt trapped! I scanned the landscape for a way out, and that is when I first saw them. High on the top of the cliff, and silhouetted by the bright afternoon sun, stood a big familiar horse. He was only a dark shadow. But…I knew him from somewhere, just as I instinctively knew the shadowy figure upon his back. My heart was racing. I blinked to clear my vision thinking that I was seeing strange things from looking into the sun, and sure enough upon opening my eyes again the shadow horse and his rider were gone!

I turned to ask one of the other horses if they had seen them too, but everyone was far ahead of me. I tried to refocus and concentrate on the rock strewn river bottom as I picked my way along behind the others. I can' begin to tell you how relieved I was when we found a crossing on the opposite bank.

I climbed out of that spooky place and commented to Spy, "I'm glad that we're out of there. I'm sure not looking forward to the return trip. Did you see the dark horse and rider on the top of the cliff?"

"No. I didn't notice anything, but I was watching every step on the shifting shale beneath my hooves."

" What about you, Midnight? You see another horse and rider above us?"

Midnight snorted "No." He didn't notice anyone on the top of the cliff, and what's more not one of the mares had observed anything. Why had only I see them?

An alternate return route kept us from having to traverse that section of the river again. I should have been relieved, but the shadowy figures backlit by the sun continued to haunt me. Had I really seen them? Or did I only imagine the whole experience?

Down we went into the river again. That crossing was a nice gradual slope easy to navigate. The water was dead calm, but it was deceptively deep. Water quickly swirled around my knees! I lowered my head to check it out and that was when I saw my own reflection. But something was different about the horse looking back at me. Gone was my bridle and western saddle, along with Marcie! My watery reflection had feathers in his forelock and his rider wore a long fringed buckskin shirt that was belted at the waist, a pair of leggings, a breechcloth, and plain unadorned moccasins.

That mirrored image unnerved me. I'd seen my reflection in the water many times, but I'd know that I was looking at myself because Marcie was always reflected there too. I was not sure what I just saw. I didn't mention that experience to the other horses, they were all looking at me like my brains were scrambled since I mentioned seeing the rider on the cliff above the river. For the first time, I couldn't wait to get out of the park and return home.

S SHIPLEY 76

2

Oregon 1869

Twice today I thought that I'd actually seen myself: once as my rider Standing Bear and I traversed the high ground looking for game. I'd swear I saw myself struggling to cross the river below, faint and far away, sort of a ghost image of me. The second time, I saw my reflection as I stopped to take a drink from a small northern tributary of the Snake River. I wondered if I had eaten some locoweed, and that was the reason for my strange visions. My reflection was wearing leather on his head, and a metal device in his mouth. Mounted on his back was a small pale female dressed in a most peculiar fashion. She wore dark leg coverings, a strange puffy reddish vest, and a dark head covering that had a bill like a duck! At the back of her head a tail of hair escaped from the bizarre head covering, and hung past her shoulders. Although my experience with white people was limited, I could not recall any of them dressed like the small woman astride my reflection. If this was a vision of my future, I wondered what transgression I had made to be traded to a far off-land and demoted to a woman's mount. Standing Bear nudged my sides to get me to focus on the job at hand. We were tracking an elk.

Standing Bear

"Pay attention, Nightstalker! You seem distracted today, not at all yourself. I know you're still young, and this is your first hunt, but keep your wits about you and stay alert."

I discussed my young trainee with the other hunters over the campfire that evening.

"Overall, I am very pleased with Nightstalker's strength and courage. He's surefooted, and usually his focus is unshakeable. He may just be tired like all of us."

My mind wandered as sleep refused to come. One more night will be spent in the mountains before we can return to our home in the lush Wallowa Valley. Nights are already cold up here, and we tracked through an early snowfall during the day's hunt. When we returned to our camp the other hunters and I added several mountain sheep to our growing tally; the elk that had eluded us when Nightstalker balked at something will not be a great loss, but it could have been. The travois and pack animals will be overloaded with dear, elk, caught earlier in the hunt, a couple of moose, and a brown bear that had decided to help himself to a deer that we'd hung from a tree to drain. Like us, the bear was preparing for a long winter. He was on a quest to eat as much as he could before hibernating, and had the misfortune to try stealing the dear that belonged to our hunting party. Instead of hibernating in a cave for the winter that foolish brown bear will help fill the larder of the Nimi'ipuu.

Nimi'ipuu is my peoples name for themselves. The pale faces call our people Nez Perce. Most of us live in small bands that are usually extended family units. Our band makes our home near the Snake River.

We took turns watching over our horses, and protecting our precious winter stores. Sleep never came to me before my turn at sentry duty that night. My father had taught me to hunt and to keep vigilant. He'd warned me, "Old or injured predators unable to catch their own game will often try to sneak up close to camp looking for the right opportunity. Mountain lions, bears, and occasionally wolves follow our hunting parties. They are attracted by the smell of the fresh kills, and driven by hunger."

Their plight is understandable, but people who steal, I can't understand. My father once told me, "Men of honor do not take from those who have worked hard to supply stores for their families. Men who steal are just mean and selfish, or too lazy to hunt for themselves."

Voices from the hunters drifted to where I was grazing. I couldn't hear what they were saying, but I had a bad feeling that Standing Bear was talking about me again and this time it wasn't praise.

When I was just a foal my mother, Starlight, told me, "It pays to be vigilant son." I was grateful for the clear sky and the bright moonlight, I carefully munched on grass, making sure to avoid any suspicious plants that I wasn't familiar with. Strange visions, or a foggy mind was the last thing that I wanted. My goal was to remain clearheaded and ready for action.

Fortunately, that night, thieves, human or hungry predators, did not attack us. Snow flurries greeted us as we prepared to break camp the following morning. My first extended hunt was coming to an end. It had lasted ten long days. I'd only been on one-day searches for small game until this hunt. Once we left the mountain and the tall trees behind, our riders removed the gloves that they had pulled on before dawn. The sun was high when we neared home, and the hunters also shed their bison skin robes.

Standing Bear placed his discarded robe across my withers, and I could feel the tension leave him as his legs relaxed against my sides. I too breathed a lot easier. Before us stretched miles of sweet prairie grass that I knew didn't hide any weeds that could mess with a horse's mind. Standing Bear and the other hunters were relieved because it would be difficult for an enemy, or a determined animal to sneak up on us. Our home in the valley afforded us an unobstructed view across the prairie. I was born here, a little over four years ago, and this was home.

Our homecoming was joyful. We were greeted, like returning heroes, with much happiness and love by the hunters' families and the rest of the people. I was horse-napped almost immediately by Standing Bear's young brother, Little Wolf. I had been given to him after a harrowing swim in icy waters when I was just two. Two more years had passed since my fateful dip in the swift flowing river, and Standing Bear was working on my training as a valuable part of their extended family.

I will never forget my first encounter with Little Wolf. My mind traveled back to the time before he adopted me, or maybe it was I who adopted him.

Nez Perce horse herd 1865

The first year of my life was pretty uneventful, and I stayed close to my mother for the first few months. At that time, my life consisted of playing with the other foals; we ran and ran. We raced one another around the proximity of our mothers. We grew strong and fleet on the sweet grass near the sparkling waters that ran close to our summer home. Mock battles became a favorite sport for us colts, but the fillies didn't care to romp with us much anymore. The more rowdy we became the less we saw of the fillies our age. Their mothers warned them to stay away from us, and they obeyed without question.

Young riders were assigned to patrol our herd, and at night their number would increase. The air became cool, and ice began to form along the edge of the river. That was the first year I made the trip to our winter home, guided by the sentries who protected us from predators and horse thieves. We traveled north along the Snake River closer to the windbreaks provided by the tall trees and the closer proximity of the great mountains. I learned the function of the guards from my mother; she was just loaded with information. Her coat was darker than mine, but she had many white spots over her entire body.

We returned each spring in time for the salmon run; it was amazing to see the large fish jump into the air as they struggled against the swift flowing current to swim upstream! I was two now and had seen the big salmon twice on our return to our summer place. I still can't figure out why they don't just swim with the direction the water flowed. That always worked for us horses when we had to ford a swift river.

The moving process was quite an undertaking. Everything was packed for the seasonal journey. Tepees were dismantled and loaded on packhorses and onto travois, along with every cooking pot and other personal belonging. Babies were strapped on cradleboards that were securely attached to their mother's back, or to the front of the saddle of a mother's astride horses. The cattle herd traveled in a closely packed bunch, much the same as we did. We were allowed to spread out to graze under the watchful eyes of our night guards whenever the people made camp for the night.

Spring 1867

That year we'd been back only a short time when I had my first run-in with horse thieves. We were grazing under the skimpy light provided by a sliver of a new moon. I new that something wasn't right when I found one of our guards, Sundown, sprawled out the ground, and I almost stepped on him! He let out a groan just in time. I peered into the night looking for his patrol horse. He was missing, along with Starlight and my new little sister. I heard my mother call out to her foal "come to Mommy little girl!"

I didn't know what to do, so I whinnied to the rest of the herd, "Danger! Someone attacked Sundown and took his horse, my mom, little sister, and maybe others, too!"

I took off in the direction that I heard my little sister crying. Her mostly white coat would have been hard to miss on a brighter night, but the dark night wasn't going to protect her from hungry predators if she kept whinnying so loudly.

I caught up with her quickly. "Hush, little one. Unless you want to be a late night snack for wolves."

She was trembling with fear. "Mommy's gone, I can't find her, or even hear her anymore!"

"Come with me, quickly. I will get you back to safety. Then I will go find our mother."

"You promise to find Momma?"

"I promise. Hurry, now, before they get too far ahead."

The little one was tired and weak. It took longer than I would have liked to get her back to the herd. When I returned with my little sister, a party of six warriors was already mounted on big strong warhorses who were unknown to me at that time. They were prepared to hunt down whoever had taken our mother. A guard of sixteen earth years, whom later I found out was called *Standing Bear*, slipped a horsehair rope over my little sister's neck and nose; then he coaxed her back to the people's lodgings. The little one was in safe hands, so I spun around and took off after the hunting party. I was determined to find my mother and bring her back.

One of the warriors had dismounted to check for tracks in the inky night. I whizzed past them and nickered low to the other horses as I went by, "Follow me! I know which way they went."

The tracker on the ground seemed to understand, for he leapt back on his horse, and in no time the big powerful full-grown horses were hot on my tail. About an hour later I came to a halt and almost got run over! I didn't think to give advance warning before stopping so quickly in the dark.

"Are you trying to end your life so soon, kid?" one of the stallions behind me nickered in a slightly perturbed voice.

"I heard something. Listen!" I stood still for a few seconds listening to sounds in the night, and catching my wind. Then I heard it again! It was Starlight. I took off, my hooves eating up the ground between my mother and me. I guess the sound of my mother's distressed voice lent wings to my hooves; I exploded back into a run leaving the older horses in my wake. I entered a stand of trees in the heat of the chase. It was even darker in the forest than it was out on the open field. If I'd been older and smarter, I would have waited for my reinforcements.

It came as a shock to me that the thieves were very much like our people. But they wore their hair differently and had different paint on their bodies. My mother was putting up a fuss, making it impossible for the thief leading her to keep up with the others who were now moving faster, attempting to escape the thundering hooves coming behind me. Mom's horsenapper was bringing up the rear. I barreled up behind him and bit the Pinto stallion he was riding as hard as I could, smack on his big butt, then yelled, "Run, Mom!"

The Pinto's rider had his hands full controlling the stallion that was now intent on retaliating and taking a piece out of me. The young brave lost the hold he had on my mom, but instead of making a run for it Starlight joined in the fray. The shout and following string of nasty words from the first horse thief we'd neutralized caused the next one in the group to stop. He turned around to check out the alarmed voice of our adversary.

I focused my attention on him and charged forward applying my teeth again, this time to the rider's leg. While I was inflicting some serious hurt on the second horse thief, Mom whipped around to the rear and bit his sorrel gelding on the hind end. Yep. You guessed it; one more of their captive horses was freed.

That was the end of our heroics. The warriors and their horses thundered past Mom and me and made quick work of subduing the remainder of the raiders. As it turned out the thieves were young braves from another tribe that were longtime adversaries of the Nez Perce people and they were engaging in a ritual called *counting coup*. The rescuers recovered four more members of our herd, including the one who belonged to the injured Sundown.

Starlight was in a hurry to get back to find her foal.

"Relax, Mom, I already found her. She's back home in the care of the people."

"You are very brave for one so young, my son. The thieves never saw you coming, you were like a shadow horse!"

You wouldn't think that the stoic warriors would be prone to gossip, would you? Well, think again. Apparently, the young raiders were out of luck, in more ways than one. Bragging rights for counting coup required that the enemy not be injured; the inexperienced braves messed that one up by hurting Sundown. Also, for a successful coup, it was required that the raiders themselves return uninjured. Well…the raider on the Pinto stallion got a bad headache from colliding with a tree while trying to regain control of his horse, and the second brave I'd encountered sported a set of nasty looking teeth marks.

Of course part of the story telling was because in a strange turn of events, thanks to yours truly, our warriors did successfully count coup! What happened next that night took me by surprise. Our warriors tied the thieves to their own horses—but facing backwards—and sent them on their way. My guess is, to be found this way brings great shame upon the brave and his family. Eagle feathers were awarded to the six rescuers to symbolize their successful coup.

Once word got around of my so-called heroics, everyone had to come by to look at me. The adults didn't see anything special. But the children came up with the rumor that I only showed my special talents at night. They began to sneak away from camp after dark to seek me out. It became a game with them to see whether or not I could disappear into the darkness.

I was just as curious about them, so I would sneak up behind them and snort. Some of the children would giggle, and others would run off making squealing noises. Some nights the lights from the campfires would reflect in my eyes. The children swore to their parents that my eyes changed to hot glowing coals when darkness blanketed the land. Their tale was that I turned into a shadow warrior and stalked the night. Yep. At the age of two I earned my descriptive name. "I was called the Nightstalker from then on.

Enough of the background stuff; back to the meeting with Little Wolf. His then twelve-year-old sister, Songbird, was given the chore of looking after him one afternoon while their mother gathered berries. Songbird had her hands full and promised Little Wolf that she would take him that night to see the shadow horse, Nightstalker, only if he'd behave for her. The child was just six that spring, and he still believed in all the legends and ghost stories told by the people. That night was another dark one, making me hard to see, and my eyes caught the firelight. All that Little Wolf saw were two glowing orbs moving toward him in the darkness, and he let out a howl that would have put a full-grown wolf to shame. He sure scared the poop out of me! I'd had more than enough of that game for the night.

Songbird must have squealed on her little brother. The next day, all the other children were teasing him relentlessly. Standing Bear took matters into his own hands and brought his little brother to see me in the daylight. Like I said before I'm not spectacular by the light of day, nor at all frightening. I was just another young colt with a dark coat, a small star, a sock on my right ankle, snowflakes on my rump, and black spots that were barely visible under my dark coat. In the winter I was almost black and my dark spots were invisible.

Standing Bear inched his sibling closer, and Little Wolf reached out his small hand. I lowered my head to get a better look at this small human. My first whiff of him told me he was the howler from a few nights ago. He petted my nose with his small pudgy hand and then declared, "*Mine!*"

He came to see me every day, after that. An older family member accompanied Little Wolf on most of his visits, but sometimes he'd steal away and visit me by himself.

Several days of heavy rain kept him confined. The rain was not very cold, but it melted much of the snow that was still high in the mountains. Melting snow increased the current of the river until it overflowed the banks. Mares wisely moved their foals farther from the rising water. On the first sunny day, Little Wolf had escaped the watchful eyes of his mother and grandmother to come for an overdue visit. I heard cries of panic from the village, and turned to investigate the ruckus. The two women suddenly noticed that their charge was on the run toward the river. On most visits he came along a path that ran parallel to the river, but on that day the path was under water.

I watched the human drama as his mother ran to save her child from certain doom. The rascal took one look at his mother chasing after him, giggled, and picked up speed. I heard his mother let out a terrified screech when her son slipped and fell into the raging water. At that point, I galloped as fast as I could to intercept the rambunctious little boy. He was able to grab hold of a partially submerged tree limb. His presence of mind allowed me the time I required. I plunged into the icy river and battled the current to reach him. I was becoming winded and my heart was pounding against my ribs as I swam upstream.

"Almost there, just a few more feet," I told myself as my strength threatened to fail me. I was so close. Then the child lost his grip! He began tumbling in the water and was headed in my direction. His little hand found purchase in my mane when he collided with me. The little imp scrambled onto my back and held to my mane for dear life.

I fought the powerful current to reach dry land, but I sank to my knees on a bank that usually provided good footing. Little Wolf's frantic mother was just barely able to reach out and pluck him from my back.

The women's screams had caught the attention of the others in the village. I was becoming exhausted and the more I struggled, the deeper in the muck I sank. Two ropes tossed around my neck helped keep me from sinking lower, but I didn't have the strength left to help myself.

When Standing Bear arrived, he jumped into the muck and began to scoop the mud away from me while I regained my wind. Soon other men joined him; they worked to remove the suction that'd bogged me down. Many warriors pitched in to dig me out; some of them pushed on my rump, and others pulled on the ropes around my neck. With a concerted effort, I was able to get purchase onto dry ground. I'd rescued Little Wolf, but Standing Bear and the rest of the people had saved me.

I was escorted to the family's teepee lodge where Standing Bear cleaned the mud from my coat, rubbed me down, then covered me with warm woven blankets. They felt strange on my back, but the blankets warmed me. Soon the shivering in my body stopped. My legs still felt weak, and I wondered if Little Wolf felt as cold and weak as I did. I lay down to rest next to the family lodge.

That's how I became a member of the family. I already knew Standing Bear, Little Wolf, and Songbird, but I got to meet the rest of the family while the trouble prone child and I recuperated from our ordeal in the swift flowing floodwaters. Spotted Elk was their father and one of the tribal elders. Their mother's name was Wind Song, and their grandmother was called Speckled Bird. They all took turns tending to me. I recovered sooner than Little Wolf. He was battling something called pneumonia. I worried about him. Even after I was returned to the herd, I wandered into the village to visit with him and check on his progress.

Standing Bear was given the job of training me the following year, because Little Wolf was still too young. It was understood by the entire tribe that I was eventually to be Spotted Elk's youngest son's horse. Whenever my lessons or hunting trips were completed, Little Wolf would jump on my back and howl like a fierce warrior. He called me his great shadow warhorse, and warned his pretend enemies to beware of him and his Nightstalker.

Standing Bear

There has been some contention among the representatives of some of the other bands with whom we trade horses. Word of the young stallion Nightstalker has traveled like a bird in flight. They were here to trade broodmares, colts, and trained warhorses, whatever it took to take the young stallion home. Courage and endurance were prized above all else, and to make matters worse, Nightstalker was put together very well and showed promise of being a big powerful horse.

The problem arose when my father offered them the choice of any two-year-old stallion except Nightstalker. The council of elders had decided that the colt would be given to Little Wolf. The other horse breeders were outraged and could not understand the waste of a potentially great breeding sire. They knew that a horse destined for a child could not remain a stallion.

3

Olmsted Falls, Ohio 1970

I have a new trail buddy. His name is Joey, and he is also an Appaloosa. Joey's owner, Terrie, and Marcie have become friends. As a result of their friendship, Joey and I spend a lot of time together. He is a year younger than me and had very little handling when he arrived at Hi-Lo last fall. Joey doesn't have the stocky build that I have. He's kind of tall and lanky, more like a young Thoroughbred racehorse. His color is a bright sorrel with a blazed face and a large white hip blanket.

Terrie lives just up the road from Hi-Lo and walks to the barn every day. We had a new adventure when our humans took us on the road together for the first time. We hoofed over to Terrie's parents' house, trotted around in their backfield for a while then it was back to Hi-Lo. The next time we also took a gallop down the long dirt road across from Terrie's home.

We repeated the spin around that backyard a few more times before our graduation to the dirt access road across the street. We were just loping along, minding our own business and enjoying the long straightaway, when a two-wheeled contraption came roaring up next to us. The young rider challenged Terrie to a race. Joey was dancing around, nervous-like.

"What's that loud noise, Frosty?"

"I don't know, Joey." I was as puzzled as he was. "I never heard a bicycle make noise like that!"

Marcie told me what it was. *Easy, Frosty, it's just a bike with a motor called a motorcycle.* Marcie often talked to me like I could understand every word that she said. In truth, it was her calm manner, and the quiet confident sound of her voice that always reassured me.

The next thing I knew Joey's hooves were flying down the road next to the cycle and he was pulling away from the machine until the dirt road dead-ended into a paved cross street. Terrie and he came to a screeching halt at the end of the dirt road! The cyclist turned to the right and roared up the paved road.

When we caught up I was as surprised as Marcie at how fast Joey could run.

"Wow! That was some race, Joey," I exclaimed.

"I wasn't racing that noisy contraption, I was trying to run away from it!" he said, shaking out his mane.

"Well…truth be told, I think Terrie was making a race out of it.

"Maybe," Joey concurred. "She sure didn't try to slow me down!"

Terrie was seventeen and still in 4-H so we began to ride over to her club leader's farm once a week for workouts. I was getting pretty good at this road riding stuff. Neither of our owners had a horse trailer. As our riders included the three-mile weekly road trips into the park to the mile and a half 4-H jaunt we became seasoned road warriors.

Early that fall, we had to take a detour because our usual route was torn up. Marcie called it *roadwork*. That's how we ended up waiting for a freight train at a railroad crossing.

Our manes picked up the cool breeze and flipped around our necks while we waited for the endless procession of train cars to pass by. Huge boxes on wheels and flat beds with lumber or coils of steel clanked and rumbled past us.

Strong tremors shook the soles of my hooves and traveled up my legs; my heart began to pound like a war drum. Marcie stroked my neck and held me a safe distance from the metal monster. Joey was very frightened and was looking to me for guidance.

"Frosty, aren't you scared?" he whinnied.

I couldn't lie to him, so I chose my answer carefully. "Joey, are we not descendants of the fabled warhorses of the Nez Perce?"

My tactic worked. Joey perked his ears, puffed out his chest, and turned to face the terrifying beast. The kid stood his ground, and he made every attempt to look brave and strong.

Once the train passed, we watched as a parade of cars and trucks rumbled over the tracks from both directions. Our riders continued to hold us back until there was a break in the traffic. We were finally given the cue to move. I stepped from the side of the paved road onto the thick plank surface that anchored the rails for the snake-like beast. I was sure I'd encountered a similar beast, but I couldn't remember where or when.

Joey breathed a big sigh of relief. "I sure like it better when we can hitch a ride with the other horses in their trailers, Frosty."

"Yeah, I didn't like that train thing much either."

Joey settled down quickly once we entered the park. The warm afternoon sun filtered through the canopy of brightly colored trees, and the fall of leaves formed a brilliant layer over the bridle path. We followed the multicolored ribbon winding among the tree-covered hills.

"I think the red leaves crunch better than the orange or gold ones." Joey then tried to prove his point by lifting his feet a little higher so the leaves crackled louder beneath his hooves. He was clearly enjoying himself. I had this nagging feeling that making noise was not a good thing, and I walked softly.

We only occasionally tossed our heads or flicked our tails at a determined fly. The cool fall air kept most of the flies away and they did not annoy us as much as they had during our summer trail rides.

Joey was always happier when we had some speed going. He would pull on this bit. "Let's run!" he snorted and tossed his head impatiently.

"You can't run all the time, Joey," I laughed.

"Why not?"

How was I supposed to answer that? Jogging and loping were just not Joey's style.

We again approached the train crossing on our return trip home. The muscles began to twitch beneath my skin, and the twitching didn't have a thing to do with dislodging another fly. I tried to focus on the task at hand, but my skin felt prickly the way it always did before one of my visions. The residual tremors from a recently passed train changed its cadence. I scoured the landscape looking for a heard of great shaggy cow-like creatures that shook the earth when they ran. Marcie stroked my neck, and her voice brought me back from the edge before I could slip into that other strange world.

4

1870
Where are the buffalo?

Standing Bear and Sundown

"Nightstalker's life will change dramatically this year, Sundown, he is now a mature horse of five years."

"I think life is going to change for all of us, Standing Bear. Tensions are escalating between our people and the white settlers. They just move in and build homesteads on our ancestral lands. That's bad enough, but when our leaders try to make peace and coexist with the white invaders they have once again been rebuffed. Many among the settlers are greedy. They rustle our people's cattle, and raid our horse herds."

"They are wily thieves that's for sure. They only steal the solid colored horses from among the herds of our people. Plain colored horses can easily pass for their own stock. Once they put their brand on our stolen cattle and horses, marking them as their property, there is little our leaders can do to prove they were stolen from among the Nez Perce herds."

"My mistrust of the pale faces is growing, my friend. Not only have they stolen from us but an increasing number of our people have been killed by these invaders in the last ten years, and more and more of the white plague is spreading across our land."

"I know. My father was returning from a council gathering at Indian Town when his great warhorse Thunderbird was shot from under him. We were on our way home from the meeting with representatives from other Nez Perce

bands. The Council was to decide on a strategy to deal with the hordes of whites invading our homes. I saw Thunderbird go down. At first, I feared my father was also dead. I pulled Spotted Elk up behind me, and Yellow Jacket, here," he paused long enough to stroke his horse's glossy golden neck, "carried us both home. We were all upset at the loss of Father's great horse and very angry at the unprovoked attack."

"I was surprised that with only a few relatively small game hunts to Nightstalker's credit that your father has picked the gelding as his mount for the hunt in buffalo country."

Nightstalker

I was so excited! Spotted Elk had been riding me lately, and he has chosen me to go on a buffalo hunt on the Great Plains east of our home. The creatures that I'd yet to see roamed the land of our trading and hunting partners the Crow. I overheard that some tribes of the Lakota people also called that land home.

Once everyone had arrived at the gathering site and set up camp, scouts were sent out from each of the tribes participating in the hunt to locate the herd. I listened in to the human conversations, taking in what little I could understand of the different and strange speech of our hunting partners. It was Yellow Jacket, Standing Bear's buckskin stallion, who shed the most light on what we were looking for.

He was a colorful guy: his golden dappled coat glistened in the sunlight. His white blanket covered most of his upper back and rump where it almost dipped to meet his black legs just above the hocks. His black legs, mane, tail, black rimed ears, and white blanket loaded with spots aside, the most striking thing about him was his white rimed hazel eyes!

"On my first hunt, Nightstalker, the buffalo were easy to find. They dotted the plains as far as I could see. Today they were much harder to locate, and the herd was much smaller."

"What do they look like?" I asked.

"Buffalo are great shaggy beasts, most are brown, but once in a great while a white one will appear. The white buffalo are very rare and are sacred to many of the tribes of the plains. There are sharp curved horns on the head of the adults. One swipe of those powerful horned heads can rip a horse open and send his rider catapulting beneath their equally deadly hooves."

"How do you keep from getting gored?"

"Run fast and straight, Nightstalker, when your hunter picks his buffalo. Put him in a position to make a clean kill! If he misses with his spear and the bull makes a move to attack, get out of the way. I don't think you need to worry much. Spotted Elk is one of the best and I've never seen him miss. Just remember: some of the bulls weigh well over a ton, that's more than twice our weight!"

I couldn't think of another thing to say. I just prayed to the Great Spirit that I was up to the task.

We worked our way toward the herd of buffalo from downwind. I followed the lead of the experienced horses and was glad that Spotted Elk was an old hand at this. His calm attitude helped settle me, and I walked softly making sure not to give away our position.

It was the job of some of the younger braves to ride on the opposite side of the grazing beasts making plenty of noise. Sundown was in the company of the young braves brandishing blankets as they ran their horses at the herd. To me it sounded like a competition to see which of them could make the loudest most fearsome war cries. The ruckus sent the buffalo on the run toward the hunters.

I noticed that the large bulls moved to the edge of the stampeding throng. Mothers with calves and the very young were clustered at the center of the thundering herd.

Spotted Elk set me into a run parallel to the herd. He'd picked his buffalo, and asked me for more speed. Yellow Jacket's advice replayed in my mind. *"Run fast and straight, Nightstalker, when your hunter picks his buffalo."*

For big cumbersome-looking animals, the shaggy American Bison were fast and very agile. I really had to hustle to stay along side the selected bull. Next thing I knew, Spotted Elk's lance sent the bull tumbling to the ground. He pushed me away with his leg and we slowed to

an easy lope. We would have to wait for the rest of the herd to pass to retrieve his lance and claim our buffalo.

Standing Bear and Yellow Jacket were behind us and on the other side of the herd. At age nineteen, that was only Standing Bear's third hunt and he ended up with two buffalo! Prior to his first official hunt, the young brave had been one of the noisy chasers. Sundown's old patrol partner had just gone to sleep one night and never woke up, and his new horse was still too young to hunt buffalo. So he brought up the rear with the howling younger braves.

As we grazed under the stars near the camp where the warriors were celebrating a good hunt, I questioned Yellow Jacket: "How did you and Standing Bear bring down two buffalo?"

"Standing Bear had selected an aged bull that didn't drop immediately. It slowed some then took aim at us, but the Great Spirit was watching over us. A younger bull that we would not have selected for the hunt ran smack into him! The two bulls got tangled up and run over by a few of their herd mates. Once the herd passed Standing Bear used his bow on the injured younger bull. It's hard to say whether his broken leg was the result of the entanglement with the larger bull or one of the others that stepped on him. Either way, the result was the same, he wouldn't have been able to survive, but he saved us. For that Standing Bear said a prayer of thanks to the young one's spirit."

"Wow! That was quite a near miss! I am glad that the Great Spirit was watching out for both of you." I didn't tell Yellow Jacket, but I was feeling much better about my one and only buffalo.

We brought home enough meat to be cured that would last our human family through the winter. The hides would make warm robes and blankets; some parts would be tanned for other uses. There was no part of a buffalo the tribes couldn't find a use for.

Back home

After we returned from the hunt, Spotted Elk was dividing his training expertise between a young stallion named White Cloud and me. You guessed it! White Cloud was the complete opposite of me, snow white with a small black spot here and there. He kind of reminded me of my little sister, the one I had rescued years ago from the horse thieves, though she had many more spots. My sister and some of the other fillies were traded to other bands for use as broodmares. The people would not breed daughters back to their sires. To keep the horse herd strong, sons of the herd sire were also either gelded or traded off to other Nez Perce horse breeders. I was gelded because I was to be Little Wolf's horse, but because of my strength, speed, and courage I was trained as a warrior's horse. It worried me some that I would be left behind on the next trip to the eastern plains for buffalo. However, White Cloud wasn't far enough along in his training to replace me, yet.

Standing Bear and Sundown were each assigned several young horses to break and train; both were exceptional riders and trained many horses for the people's use and for trade. Sundown, more so than Standing Bear, stuck like a burr to the bucking horse's backs.

Sundown had named his white speckled bay stallion Hopper. He'd earned the name from his habit of crow hopping whenever he got excited!

For the second year in a row Spotted Elk chose me as his hunting partner. It was taking longer to find the herds than it did the year before. One of the Crow horses told us, "The herds are being killed in mass numbers by white men, called buffalo hunters, and they use loud fire sticks to bring down the buffalo. They are much bigger and louder than the rifles used by some of our warriors. The coldhearted white hunters only take the hides; the rest of the felled beasts are left to rot."

Yellow Jacket and I found that hard to believe until we saw it for ourselves while searching for the herds.

Everyone was sad, and angered about the senseless waste. The lighthearted mood of the previous year was absent from this hunt.

I didn't go with Spotted Elk and Standing Bear on the next two buffalo hunts.

Little Wolf was promoted in status shortly after his twelfth birthday ceremony. When I returned from my trip to the plains, where the dwindling buffalo herds roamed, we were assigned a new task. Little Wolf was now given the duty of horse wrangler. He and I joined the slightly older daytime guards to learn what was required to guard the horse herd. Night duties fell to the older braves.

Little Wolf and I were allowed to join in an exhilarating gallop with his father and brother. Little Wolf was not permitted to go alone to provide the conditioning that I required. Things were deteriorating in the negotiations with the white chiefs in a place called Washington.

I did not have any idea where this place was, so on one of our outings I asked Yellow Jacket as we walked side-by-side back to the village.

"I don't know where it is either, Nightstalker. Only that it is many days east of where the buffalo live."

"If they are so far away, why are the elders concerned about the white chiefs?"

"Battles have broken out in the land of the Lakota and Cheyenne. The white invaders and their chiefs lump all Native People together. When one tribe makes trouble the whites, in their ignorance, blame our people too."

Little Wolf went on his first hunt for deer, elk, mountain sheep, and smaller game. I was an old pro at game hunting by that time. We helped bring home stores to supplement the buffalo meat: salmon, trout, and other fish. What was not consumed while fresh was dried and stored for the long winter. I would often catch a whiff of the wild onions, wild carrots, and herbs the women gathered during the growing season as they bubbled in the cooking pots. The wild carrots make my mouth water;

Little Wolf had been giving me a taste as a treat ever since he recovered from the sickness after our frightening swim in the flooded river.

* * *

The buffalo hunt of 1875 started out badly. Just before the hunters were to leave a crazed bear attacked Standing Bear and Yellow Jacket. Spotted Elk and Standing Bear were able to kill the bear, but it had clawed a deep wound in Yellow Jacket's right shoulder. My buckskin friend would take much tending and time to recover. It was impossible for him to travel to the plains for the hunt, so I was pressed into service as his replacement.

That seemed to be my function in life, to protect the herd and Little Wolf, and be ready to step in to replace an injured friend. I prayed that Yellow Jacket wouldn't be joining the great Thunderbird anytime soon.

Little Wolf was always telling me, "*Nightstalker, brave warriors and brave horses will go to the Happy Hunting Ground of their ancestors. If they were very brave in this life, the Great Spirit may give them another chance at life.*"

I wondered if this was a little known fact, a story to motivate children to behave, or just something that Little Wolf invented. He had quite an imagination!

He was not very happy about using one of the other geldings to carry out his guard duties, but he wished his father and brother a successful hunt. Before we left he gave me a wild carrot, and said, "*Be safe my Shadow Warrior, and bring my family back home. You are the bravest horse that ever walked our land.*"

"Wow! That kid can sure spin some tall tales, and it looks like he goes overboard with the complements too," White Cloud commented as we left camp.

"He's still a child that remembers the tales of the shadow horse, and my swim in the floodwaters to rescue him, so he exaggerates my prowess."

"I should say he does!" White Cloud snorted.

I ignored his sarcastic remark, and concentrated on the descent from the mountains that separated our home and the plains. I sure missed

Yellow Jacket, and wondered how he had tolerated White Cloud on the past two hunts. I was ready to kick the daylights out of him. What a pain in the butt!

We met with hunters from several other Nez Perce bands along the way. Fewer of the Crow hunters joined us than had when I was part of the hunt three years ago. Instead of the young warriors of the Lakota, the hunter's were more of Spotted Elk's generation, and some looked like grandfathers with much gray streaked through their braids. The young warriors were protecting the villages from hostile white men. Some of their horses looked to be as aged as their riders, but they were a wealth of information.

White Cloud was skeptical of some of their exploits. I didn't say anything; I remembered the disbelief that I had on my second hunt when the Crow horse told me about the mass killing by the white buffalo hunters. I had to see it to believe. The horse gossip this hunt was about a great snake-like creature that belched thick black smoke into the sky and rode parallel rails that now bisected their human counterpart's lands and hunting grounds.

Hopper sidled up to me and said, "Do you believe their strange tales, Nightstalker?"

"I don't totally disbelieve. They live here and should know, but I sure hope they are exaggerating."

White Cloud just snorted to show his usual skepticism. "Of course, it's just a tale to scare twits like the two of you."

He was really testing my temper. "Take a hike, Whitey, our low mentality might be catchy."

Hopper snorted a couple of times to contain his laughter. He didn't want to offend the older stallion, but I didn't care so much. White Cloud lorded it over us because Spotted Elk had chosen him to replace the legendary Thunderbird.

I pinned my ears back and dared him to make a move at me. Stallion or not, I knew that I could take him any day of the week!

Standing Bear

We were part of one of the scouting parties looking for the elusive buffalo. We'd tracked a small herd, less than fifty, including the cows and calves. Little Eagle one of the Crow scouts told us, "We need to move the herd. They're grazing too close to the iron rails! Hurry, follow me!"

Sundown and I moved our horses down the slope right behind Little Eagle. Sundown said, "The reflective rails are drawn across the land for as far as I can see in both directions!"

Little Eagle's concern soon became evident. The train appeared like great iron beast on the horizon. We hurried down to haze the buffalo away, but they'd also spotted the danger and were on the run.

The rumbling of the iron monster shook the ground, drowning out the vibrations of the stampeding herd. I pulled Nightstalker to a stop, and along with the others we watched helplessly as the slaughter began.

Instead of running at an angle, the buffalo herd tried to run ahead of the threat, too close to the rails that allowed great grooved metal wheels to propel the smoke-belching iron steam beast forward at speeds that I hadn't encountered before.

Nightstalker

I began to tremble as I struggled to catch my breath and make sense of the terrifying sight. Standing Bear tried to calm me, but I could sense that he was upset, too. The iron beast passed the herd apparently without incidence, but as it turned out, it was not the head of the snake that was dangerous. Bright flashes and loud cracking sounds coming from its sides were what began to drop the great buffalo. They finally, sensed their jeopardy and turned to run away from the tracks. But the end of the train had a platform where men with long fire sticks took aim at the retreating herd. They shot the mothers, the young calves, and killed all the bulls regardless of their maturity. I knew the white buffalo hunters were wasteful, but this I could not comprehend. The snake was gone and in its wake were dead and mortally injured buffalo. There was no honor in their deed. The cries of the injured and dying calves will echo in my ears for a long, long, time.

Standing Bear

One of the other Crow scouts had left the carnage and brought back the rest of the hunters. The other scouts, plus Sundown and I, had put the injured out of their pain, by the time my father and the others arrived. Had we not been there to witness their death, the whole herd would have just rotted under the hot sun. They would have been unfit for anything but meat for the vultures already circling.

"Have you ever seen anything like this?" I asked my father.

No, my son, I haven't. The Native People never kill the cows or the young. They're needed to perpetuate the herd. The merciless white men on the train were just having sport, with no care for the consequences of their actions."

We went to work salvaging the meat from the hapless herd, but there was none of the laughter and joyous celebration that had accompanied previous hunts.

Many of the buffalo were so young and small that a further hunt was necessary. The next day we divided what little was found that could be harvested. We'd found another herd, a larger one, that had been killed the same way and left to rot days before. I've never seen grown warriors weep, but tears fell like rain with the knowledge of the pending extinction of the once abundant buffalo. Tears welled in my father's eyes, and mine rained down my face. Soon my grief was replaced by a deep rage that was foreign to me.

"This will be the last buffalo hunt for our people," my father informed me.

A chill washed over me as I heard the talks of war around the campfire. The old Lakota warriors spoke of an impending alliance between Crazy Horse and Sitting Bull to drive the whites from their lands by eliminating the blue-coated soldiers that protected them.

We loaded the packhorses and travois for the long trip home. The future was ominous for Native Peoples. We had waited too long to repel the white invaders that plundered our land and killed only for sport. I was leaning more and more toward those who believed the whites were intent on making us as nonexistent as the disappearing buffalo, and that war was inevitable.

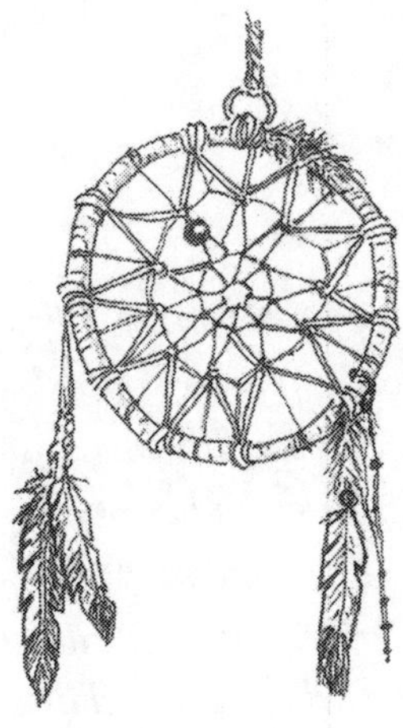

5

George's Letter to Vietnam

September 28, 1968
To: Airman Bernard Thompson
Ben Wahb Air Force Base

Hey Ben,

As promised, here's an update. It is strange being stateside again after a four-year tour with the Air Force, and once more becoming a civilian. It takes some getting used to moderating my language, and making the transition from the military schedule to which I had become accustomed.

Before going home to Mom, Dad, and my pesky younger sister, I stopped off in Phoenix to see our buddy Tom. He had been discharged just before me, and there was a blonde that I'd dated that beckoned as well. I dated Peggy while I was stationed in Arizona, before my tour in Vietnam.

Well…so much for her waiting for me. Peg has married a big loudmouthed ex-Marine. I just swallowed my pride, wished Peg, Paul, and their two-year-old rug rat a happy life. After that, I rode over to see Tom. Like us he'd been an airplane mechanic working on the F-4s that filled the sky over Nam, He spent his time in-country based in Da Nang.

Tom lives on a horse and cattle ranch a few hours from where I'd just encountered my old girlfriend's new family.

I ended up staying a couple of days with him and making arrangements for the black gelding that I'd been riding during my visit to be delivered to Ohio. Joker is a rescue that Tom saved from the slaughterhouse. The Quarter Horse went lame after extensive roping and bulldogging events, so he was consigned to an auction haunted by meat buyers.

Terrie, my little sister, as you already know, is a horse nut, but I never have been what you would call a horseman. I rode livery horses a few times while I was based in Arizona, and again later when I was stationed near Amarillo.

I covertly scouted out accommodations for my new horse, and decided on a boarding stable located in the Metro Parks that would give me access to the trails. I picked up a used 65 Chevy Impala so that I could make the fifteen-mile trip to the barn, and commute to work.

I've been hired as a mechanic for one of the airlines with a hub at Hopkins International Airport. It will require some additional training. The airline fleet is a whole other animal than the fighter jets that I worked on in the Air Force.

See you next month. Let me know when you catch a flight in.

George.

November 1970

I slapped Ben on the back when he came through the walkway at Hopkins. It was good to see his lanky form, red hair, twinkling blue eyes, and the infectious grin on his freckled face. Still in his dress blues, we were the focus of some hostile college age people. Other than them, most other folks just ignored us.

"Hey, George, I'm starved," Ben blurted out.

I thought about it for about two seconds. "Why don't we head over to the Sky Way for some good steaks?"

We caught up over dinner.

How is your job here at the airlines working out?"

"The job's okay. It and my horse keeps me out of the house most of the day and into the late evening."

"Are you avoiding your family, George?"

"Not entirely, but I haven't told my them about my horse, yet."

"Why not?"

"Joker is my quiet time, and the long trail rides relive a lot of my stress. He also allows me to avoid my matchmaking sister."

"Is she still after you to meet her friend, Marcie?"

"Oh yeah, and I decided the best way to handle it was to confront her, so I asked her, 'Terrie does your friend know that you are trying to fix her up?' She tried to change the subject, but finally stammered out, 'Well…not really. I told

her that she should meet my handsome brother when I found out you were coming home.'"

Ben laughed. "And what did Marcie say?"

"According to my sister, Marcie said that I'm too young, and she didn't have the time or inclination to train a man."

Ben grinned, shook his head and laughed at Marcie's take on men.

"I'd just laughed at her comment too, and breathed a huge sigh of relief that Marcie wasn't any more interested in getting involved than I was."

Ben set his drink down after almost choking on the last swallow. "Wait just a minute! George, did you I hear you say the word 'was' when referring to getting involved?"

"Yeah, well…fate stepped in when Marcie's car broke down. I had to go rescue not only her and Terrie but also their two horses. They'd rented a trailer and a bumper hitch to go to some horse show. Her GTO convertible staged a revolt."

"My God! George, are you sure about her? I mean, who in their right mind would pull a horse trailer with a GTO?

"You think that's unusual? Let me tell you about our strange romance. We dated a few times and I was smitten. Now I know why it didn't work out with Peggy. Marcie was waiting in my future. I proposed last month while we were parked in the drive of her parents' house, following a movie and a dinner date. She acted really surprised. And said 'Wow! George this is really unexpected.'

I said. 'Marcie, don't you feel about me the same as I do about you?' She replied, 'Yes, George, I love you too, but you know that marring me is a package deal. Frosty goes where I go. It is only fair to tell you that I won't give him up for anything.'

George shook his head. "Her loyalty and honesty amazed me, Ben."

"Well? Did you back out?"

" Heck no," I chuckled. "I agreed, and told her about Joker. I bought her a ring for Christmas, and now Marcie and I are looking for a house with some acreage, and a barn for our horses."

"Am I invited to the wedding?" was all Ben could think to say.

"Invited?" I offered my hand to seal the deal, "why, Ben, I want you to be my Best Man."

August 21, 1971 we said our vows and moved into our home, and things are never dull around our place. Frosty almost seems human at times. I often wonder if he hadn't liked me would Marcie have still married me?

6

Frosty 1972 -1976

Last August, Marcie got married, and we moved into our new home. Joey came with me. George, Marcie's new husband moved his black Quarter Horse that he calls *Joker* in at the new place too. Marcie bought a little solid bay Appaloosa filly that she named Molly. Our new barn was much smaller than what we were used to, but we were turned out most of the day. We loved being out of our stalls longer every day. I reveled in the sweet grass, as well as the shade provided by the tall trees that lined the one side of our pasture.

Our rides were different from then on, too. No more indoor arena work. We rode in the rain, the hot summer sun, and in the winter snow. I loved it, and was right at home in the changing elements.

The only thing that bothered me about my new digs was the river that ran through the back of our pasture. Most of the time it was just a quiet trickling sound, but after a big rain or snow melt it would roar like an angry beast! It brought on strange dreams that I had not experienced in nearly two years.

To add to my anxiety, Marcie rode me less and disappeared completely in the early spring. Finally, she returned, but she only came out to say hello to me and to Molly who was now officially a yearling.

George continued to turn us out and groom us the same as he had done in Marcie's absence. His sister, Terrie, who could have been his twin, helped out too. Terrie like George was tall with a flaxen mane of hair on her head, and eyes the color of a summer sky. Brother and sister were like tall thin reeds; not at all like my Marcie who fell just short of reaching George's chin.

Every now and then, I would hear a strange wailing sound from Marcie's dwelling that she shared with George.

"What is that strange noise coming from Marcie's barn?" Little Molly asked me.

Joker broke in before I could answer her, "GEORGE'S dwelling" making a point to emphasize the place belonged to George, "that he shares with Marcie is called a house."

Granted he was the oldest among us and had been on this earth four more years than the six that I had accumulated, but his stinky attitude rubbed me the wrong way.

"Okay, Mister Smarty Pants, so what is the noise that we hear?" I challenged him.

"That I do not know."

"Wow! Joker, you mean there is really something that you don't know!" Joey chimed in.

Molly giggled, and Joker snorted in disgust. I was determined to find out about Marcie's continued absence from the barn and solve the mystery of the strange noise in the house.

My opportunity came a few days later when an early spring warm spell had George leaving the large sliding door on our barn open. Once I finished my late evening grain and hay, I fiddled with my door latch until it released, then I pushed it open with my muzzle. I walked across the barn toward the open door.

"Where are you going, Frosty?" Molly nickered.

"Hush, you don't want to alert George," I scolded her. "I'm going to find out what the noise is all about."

It was pretty easy getting out of my stall, but there were two fence lines between my destination and me. The chained gate proved tamper proof, so I stuck my head out over the top fence board to gauge its height. Then, I walked back past the barn, turned to face the fence, and galloped straight at it. I sailed over the first obstacle in my path, and kept going until the second fence was also behind me. Lights from inside the dwelling helped me out as I worked my way around the house trying to peek in the windows. But the window coverings were thwarting my mission. Then I heard Marcie's voice. She sounded worried.

"George, someone is outside, prowling around the house!"

"Stay here, Marcie, I will get a flashlight, and my rifle."

I worked my way back around to the rear of the house, and was contemplating my next move when the inside door opened. Marcie let out a loud squeal, then flicked on the small back porch light. George entered the room on the run!

Then I heard Marcie yell, *"George, don't shoot! I think our prowler is Frosty. I saw his shadow when I turned on the light."*

At that point they both came out onto the back lawn where I stood rooted to the earth, like the shrubs surrounding the house. Don't ask me how I knew, but I was sure the long steel thing in George's hand was lethal. A memory from a distant past surfaced, of buffalo and my own kind dropping to the ground, never to rise again. My heart was racing even though my feet refused to move. Marcie walked up to me, rubbed my head, hugged my neck, and then scolded me.

"Frosty, you scared me out of at least ten years! I heard someone stalking around the house, and when I peered out the screen door all I could see were two glowing orbs. What are you doing out here, trying to get yourself shot?"

She had no more than asked that scary question when the strange wailing sound began again. I perked up my ears before nickering softly.

Marcie smiled, and I could see she understood me. *"Did you come to see about the crying? George, would you bring Kelly out to meet Frosty?"*

George returned a short while later without the frightening looking weapon; in its place he carried a wiggly bundle of blankets. Marcie reached over and pulled the blankets back to reveal a small human face.

"Frosty, this is Kelly, the newest member of our family."

I sniffed at the tiny human, but a pungent smell assaulted my sensitive nostrils! I backed away shaking my head and snorting. Marcy laughed at my obvious objection to the baby's odor.

"I guess Frosty is hinting that our little son needs changed."

She was still chuckling when she took the small stinky bundle from George, and walked into the house. George took me back to the barn, disconnecting the complicated chain latches on the gates. He put me in my stall and latched it again while mumbling to himself, *"I was sure that I latched all the stalls after feeding. I guess that I'll have to check the fences to see how the heck you got out, Frosty."*

George gave us some more hay and filled our water buckets; he closed all the barn doors and turned off the lights on his way out.

Molly was impatient. "What did you find out?"

"The noise that we've been hearing is a human foal. George called it a baby while he was mumbling and trying to figure out my escape route. I think the noisy newcomer belongs to Marcie and George."

A few weeks later the grass was up thick and loaded with yummy clover. Marcie was back to riding me again, but we now working in the evenings. That was the time of day when George usually returned home from what Marcie called, *His day at work.*

Our rides increased in intensity as Marcie and I got back into shape. We resumed our trail rides, and usually George rode with us. On occasion, Terrie and Joey would join us. Our first outings were in the Hinckley section of the Metro Parks. The trails that our humans chose were hilly and we had only one small creek to navigate. That suited me fine! I no longer hesitated to cross water when Marcie asked me, even if I had to swim. However, I could not shake the dread of the swift flowing streams and rivers. The water held an impending sense of doom that I didn't understand. Joker and Joey didn't mind it a bit. In fact, Joey loved to swim and play in the water!

The following spring I turned seven, by Marcie's reckoning, and Kelly turned age one four days later. So, Marcie had a big birthday bash. She even made me a horse-style birthday cake of sweet feed topped with carrot pieces.

Later that summer, after Kelly started to walk, he would toddle up to the fence, under the watchful eye of Marcie, and try to share his bottle with me whenever I moseyed over to say hello. I have to admit that these days the child smelled a lot better most of the time.

Joey and I went to a few Appaloosa shows that summer, and between classes Kelly rode in front of Marcie around the show grounds. When the leaves changed color, and began to crunch beneath our shod hooves, we traveled a long distance to a three-day Appaloosa event.

It was normal at that kind of show for me to be entered in a barrel or stake race. I was not what you would call a contest horse, but Marcie would enter to fill a class or eliminate a bye for one or both classes. When Appaloosas ran barrels, or stakes, they ran horse against horse on a mirrored image course traveling in opposite directions. It was a process of elimination requiring horses to run multiple times. The repeated runs made these classes tests of strength and agility. I usually finished in the top three. Not that I was that fast, but I didn't make mistakes, like knocking over the barrels or stakes. That particular show provided a new experience for me in the form of a steer daubing class.

Okay, the steer daubing was kind of strange. I was required to stand in a wooden chute next to a rather large steer with a big white circle painted on its middle. I waited to see what was coming next. Marcie was handed a long wooden lance with a sponge on the end that had been dipped in washable white paint. I heard a strange buzzing sound, then the steer bolted out of the open fronted stall next to me. Instantaneously, Marcie gave me a little goose with her spurs, and told me, "*Go get him, Frost!*"

I took off after the steer, and a horse's voice came to me out of the blue. *Run straight and fast, put your hunter in a good position to make a clean kill!* I blinked my eyes, for a split second the steer had transformed into a great shaggy creature! I ran alongside the strange beast, matching its every move. Marcie and I had the fastest time; our "spear" put a white blob of paint smack in the middle of the circle on that steer.

Marcie was overjoyed with me when we won the new competition. I was relieved that we didn't really kill anything, and I wondered where the voice in my head had come from.

I outdid myself in my pleasure and reining classes. Over the next day and a half, Marcie turned down several offers from other exhibitors who wanted to buy me. I was really beat when I got home from that show. After the strange voice in my head on the first day, and the memory of the domestic steer suddenly transforming into a huge shaggy beast with curved horns before my eyes, I was not about to sleep. However, images of great buffalo hunts filled my dreams once I got home and dozed off.

Joey, on the other hand, slept like an old dead log! He wasn't haunted by visions, voices, or strange dreams. He won several of his contest classes, but he didn't like the steer in the daubing class. Even though he was faster than me, he didn't have a clue how to match the steer stride-for-stride, and would overrun the target. He and Terrie ended up racing that critter around and around until the timing buzzer went off. It is never a good thing when horse and rider are not on the same page.

Terrie was doing her best to slow Joey down, but just like with the motorcycle, Joey was determined outrun the strange beast that he'd never seen before. Ranch horses dominated the daubing event, especially roping horses; the exception was yours truly.

Winter that year brought another unique experience my way. I was used to dragging logs behind me; it had been part of the trail training that Marcie taught me to increase my endurance. Instead of logs, Marcie and I began to pull a sled around in the snow while George sat on it with little Kelly in his lap. The child's delighted laughter made Marcie happy, and she praised me. Both Joey and Joker had flunked out on the empty sled pulling trials. Neither of them liked the hissing sound the sled made over the snow, and I was ordained the official family sled puller.

Right after my birthday the following spring, Marcie, George, and not-so-little Kelly went on a trip to a place called Florida. I was not really sure where that was, but they'd only been gone a couple of days when the winds howled and rattled the barn siding. The racket was deafening as rocks fell from the sky denting our metal-sided pole barn.

Molly was terrified, and the three of us macho guys tried to put her at ease by assuring her that the storm would soon pass.

Once the storm abated, Terrie came to check on us. She was house and horse sitting for my absent human family. A fallen maple tree that now blocked the driveway had just missed her car. Huge branches from other trees had crashed to earth taking down the back fence. As a result we could only go out in the smaller paddock in front of our newly pitted barn.

The rain-swollen river roared through the back pasture and echoed in my ears. I was unable to relax and graze like the others. Instead I kept a wary eye on the cresting river and swift flowing floodwaters. The rest of my barn mates didn't seem to sense the danger even as the floodwaters took over the back pasture and approached the back of our barn.

But they have never seen their own kind drowned while attempting to swim wide swift rivers. Where had that thought come from? A chill crawled along my spine, and the hair on that part of my coat stuck up like a riled porcupine!

I moved closer to the front fence gauging its height should escape become our only option. Joey, Joker, and I could probably jump it even with a short takeoff on the wet slick surface, but I wasn't so sure about Molly. Well if the worst happened, I thought that I could just push a section of the fence down. I sure wished Marcie would return. My sense of well-being was much better when she was near. I was so thankful when Marcie and George cut short their vacation and hurried home to help repair all the storm damage.

Joey left us that fall to return to Olmsted Falls. Terrie was working more hours, making it difficult for her to travel out to our neck-of the-woods. Her parents put up a barn and fenced paddock just for Joey.

The following spring I turned nine. No birthday party that year! Marcie wasn't even home, and I sure missed her. She turned up right before the human's Easter with another little bundle. This one was tiny compared to how I remember Kelly. Kara was the little human's name, and she strangely had zero hair on her head!

Okay, that explained Marcie's absence. Then less than a week later, Molly presented us with a bay filly. The little one had no face or leg markings, but she brightened the world with a huge blanket loaded with bay spots, some with darker halos.

The little one and Molly had a small sliding door on the end of their extra large stall that allowed them to go in and out at will. Mom and foal had the run of the back pasture while Joker and I were confined to the front for several months. My life brightened again when Marcie and I picked up our work routine.

We went on some trail rides over on the old Rocky River Reservation that year. Sometimes, Terrie and Joey would join us on the ride. George's parents spoiled the children while we traveled to the park. We didn't show at all that year, but the following year we were on the road nearly every weekend.

1976 was what Marcie called *the bicentennial.* She said, "*That means the United States is two hundred years old.*" I could not comprehend two hundred years, but it sounded impressive the way she said it. There were a lot of events that year that included parades, and huge horse shows where the ribbons had red, white, and blue rosettes. Often the center streamers of the ribbons also displayed the patriotic color theme, and only the side streamers identified the place. Blue for first, red for second, yellow for third place, and so on.

I got to lead several parades carrying the American flag. Joker went a few times too. He and George carried the Ohio flag, and once in a while we traded flags. Overall, the parades went off without a hitch.

At one of the big events, I believe it was called *Independence Day*, we assembled in an area near the beginning of the parade route. That part was pretty normal; the organizers gave us our positions in the parade. At the previous event, Joker and I were carrying our flags right in front of a high school marching band. My ears are still ringing!

Out of nowhere that July fourth, I experienced a strange time warp. A mounted group of Native Americans dressed in war bonnets, some wearing face paint, materialized from the direction of the parked trailers. Even some of their mounts sported war paint. That scared the poop out of me! I was terrified that I'd once more slipped the bounds of reality.

One of the war chiefs stopped to talk to George and Marcie. It was only then that I recognized his voice and the stallion he was riding from the Appaloosa show circuit a couple of years earlier. Still, when we were assigned to lead the group dressed in Native American garb, I experienced an eerie feeling of déjá-vu.

I don't know whether that parade was the big climax of the celebratory events, or Marcie had picked up on my distress and decided to put an end to our participation. Either way I was grateful. However, visions of those painted warriors and their equally fierce looking mounts preparing for battle began to reoccur in my troubled dreams.

The winter of 1976-77 kept us snowed in and close to home. Marcie and I resumed our trail riding the following summer, and all went well with the exception of my increasing terror of river crossings. Then the poop hit the fan on an early October ride.

I had a bad feeling all day about the river crossings though they were lower than normal. I hesitated at the second and widest crossing near the crossroads called *Little Cedar Point.* I'd crossed here hundreds of times, but today it really scared me. I was in the grip of a premonition when Marcie urged me forward. George and Joker were ahead of us and had negotiated the large deadfall without incidence.

I picked my way through the water and around the fallen tree. Marcie was guiding me the same way that Joker had gone. Then it hit me. *Death was imminent.* "Wait! Wait for us," I called out and moved a little faster to get to the other side of the crossing. The colorful October leaves that had been floating lazily on the surface of the river began to swirl around me, and the suddenly churned up water sucked at my legs! "Oh No!"

7

Broken Promises

Standing Bear and Sundown 1876

Sundown and I watered our horses from the bubbling waters of the Snake River on our way back to the village.

"My patience has about run out!" Sundown spat. *"I'm frustrated with our tribal elders, as are a large majority of our young Nez Perce brothers."*

"I know how you feel, Sundown. Forty of our people's chiefs and high ranking elders are still trying to negotiate with the representatives of the white settlers and ranking officers of the blue coated soldiers. Looking Glass, the Chief of our band, and several of our elders are on this last ditch effort to avoid armed confrontation with the white settlers"

"The chiefs really need to get a grip, Standing Bear. As a people, our peaceful lifestyle began to disappear with the invasion of the white homesteaders. By my fourth year on Mother Earth, the white chiefs in Washington D.C. gave the Nez Perce people the right to reside on our ancestral homelands. Many of our chiefs refused to sign the ridiculous treaty. So in the year of 1855 the pale faces successfully divided our people: those who signed the decree, and those who walked out. Our chiefs who wouldn't sign and their bands became known by the whites as the non-treaty Nez Perce."

"It didn't matter much which side of the issue the divided chiefs were on. Gold was discovered on our land in 1863 and the treaty was revoked. I also think the chiefs are fooling themselves, my friend. As the plague of white invaders spread across our land they stole our cattle, our horses, and killed

thirty of our people between 1863 and 1873. I'm sick of the white lies, injustice, and broken promises. Pale-face leaders, like the white chief Ulysses S. Grant who'd ordered that our Wallowa Valley be split between our people and the white homesteaders, spew lies with their forked tongues!"

"Hah! That didn't last long. That agreement was reached in 1873, then was revoked two years later when Grant caved to pressures of whites who wanted to settle on our land. It is only a matter of time until the blue coat soldiers try to drive us from our ancestral home. Why can't our chiefs see that?"

I sighed in resignation and shook my head in agreement. "There's no justice for our people, Sundown. And for me personally, the killing of Songbird's husband was enough for me to want revenge!" I thought about my sister's loss more and more, and the urge to seek retribution swelled within me.

Songbird had married a brave of Chief Joseph's band. Her husband was murdered while on a hunt for game during the last moon; the whites call it the month of June. Wind Blowing was smaller and more nimble than his two companions. He'd leaned his hunting rifle against the trunk as he climbed a tree to loose the deer that the braves had strung up to drain at the beginning of their hunt. He died there in that tree and toppled to the ground. Shot by an Indian hating white who was accompanying two other homesteaders. The white homesteaders claimed that they had tracked stolen horses to the camp. There were no horses in the camp, with the exception of the brave's own mounts.

The white men were named and a mock trial was held. The three white men were released, including the one who'd murdered Wind Blowing. The killer was only charged with manslaughter, and released after making a two hundred and fifty dollar bail.

Wind Blowing's companions said he was shot for pointing out, "No Nez Perce in his right mind would steal the inferior horses of the white settlers."

After killing him, the homesteaders left the hunters' camp taking their hunting rifles with them. Three days later the disputed horses were found grazing less than three miles from the owner's cabin.

The story told by Wind Blowing's two hunting partners made my stomach turn, and my blood boil!

While Joseph, and his brother Ollokot, Looking Glass, my father, Spotted Elk, and a contingent of 36 other chiefs and elders made the long trip to Lapwai to meet with the representatives of the whites and ranking soldiers, Sundown and I joined the other young braves to practice with our war lances, bows, and what few rifles we possessed. We were preparing to fight for our home.

Nightstalker

The mood of the people has changed. It had been a long bleak winter, and not much laughter came from the teepees. Even Little Wolf was subdued. The cattle herds were thinning due to the ever-increasing lack of large game. I wondered if the white men who'd slaughtered the buffalo herds, on the plains to the east, had now moved on to dear, elk, mountain sheep, and moose. More and more of the cattle went into the pot to feed the people.

The remaining cattle were moved closer to the horse herd, and guards were doubled to protect them and us from the hungry predators who had also depended on the once abundant supply of large game. Now they skulked closer and closer to our camp.

"The warriors are angry and fierce in their war games. How are you holding up, Yellow Jacket?"

"My strength has returned to almost normal, and the exercise is actually helping my recovery."

"Standing Bear appears to be one of the most fierce of the young braves," I offered.

"He is very tense and angry. His mood transfers to me and I try to be the brave fierce

warhorse that I was before the bear attacked us last year."

"You will be fine my friend, and back to your old self soon."

"I hope so. I think that I will need all my strength and courage shortly."

"Little Wolf is working my butt off too. He joins in the war games with Standing Bear and the rest of the older braves as soon as the day guards take over our duty of protecting the herd during the night."

"You know, Nightstalker, it's like the entire camp is holding their breath, waiting for the return of the elders and whatever comes next."

Standing Bear

Our mother, Wind Song, is not pleased with Little Wolf's participation in the war games. Though only fifteen he's an excellent shot with the bow and showing promise with a rifle. However, my brother lacks the strength and maturity to thrust the lance with any authority.

The return of my father and Chief Looking Glass did not bode well for our future.

My father told us, "Chief Looking Glass is not happy with your war games, and the honing of your battle skills. He's worried the whites will take the exercises as a prelude to declaring war, and he plans to order them stopped."

After relaying the chief's message, Spotted Elk in open defiance joined the young warriors. Our father shared his skills with us, and in doing so improved ours. He worked with Little Wolf until my brother could aim bow or rifle and fire with as much accuracy from Nightstalker's back at a gallop as he could from a standing or crouching position.

We spent the rest of that fall and winter improving our battle skills, and trading for more rifles. We now traveled in larger and heavier armed groups to hunt, and our band was as divided as the rest of the non-treaty Nez Perce. Negotiations had not gone well, and it was looking like we would be forced from our homes if we didn't leave on our own. Joseph, Looking Glass, and a few others were still hopeful of a last minute truce that would allow us to remain on our land.

Spotted Elk and many of the other elders believed there would be an inevitable confrontation with the whites and their soldiers. So we prepared for the worst and prayed for the best. I prayed to the Great Spirit and my ancestors; I didn't believe that the white Christian God that Chief Joseph prayed to would listen to the prayers of a red man when all the whites prayed for him to help their cause.

The hunting parties were larger that fall and many of the additional braves reminded me of the ever-vigilant herd guards. Little Wolf added a mountain sheep, one deer, six rabbits and two wild turkeys to the collective stores.

I picked up on the people's tension, and I kept alert at all times. Picketed close to our riders, Yellow Jacket and I discussed the strange atmosphere surrounding the hunt.

"I do not remember a hunt where the guards out numbered the hunters."

"It is strange, Nightstalker, that each hunter has at least one guard accompany him on his quest for game."

"Little Wolf kept grumbling in my ear that the extra guards were frightening the game away."

"I know what you mean. Whenever a guard who was busy scanning the landscape for human enemies would let his horse step on a twig, Standing Bear would growl like an angry bear. We watched helplessly as the elk that we had been tracking took off like a brown blur through the trees and thick brush. I've never seen him so angry! I thought he might turn around and unhorse his own guard!"

8

May - October 1877

Standing Bear

My father and many of the other elders had us dismantling our winter camp in the Imnaha Canyon to return to the Wallowa Valley for the spring and summer. Upon our arrival we learned that the white chiefs had sealed our destiny while we resided at our winter encampment.

Time was running out for us, our chiefs had agreed to leave the land of our ancestors and be relocated. Chief Joseph and his brother Ollokot tried to convince the blue coat, Major Woods, that we should be allowed to remain on our land, and that the Nez Perce, their name for our people, did not want to fight. In mid-May, an impatient general by the name of Howard said that negotiations were over and the reasonable time he'd given our band was up. He declared that if we remained on our land he would send soldiers to drive us from our homes.

Four other non-treaty bands of Nimi'ipuu joined with ours to make the journey to the reservation.

Nightstalker

Little Wolf and I rotated our duties between hunting for game and riding night herd over the people's ever shrinking number of cattle and the assembled band's combined horse herds.

The subdued behavior of the children was almost as spooky as the resignation and despair that I sensed in their parents and elders.

Anger over the injustice of the people's plight was growing among the young warriors. Along our journey to the west we found buffalo, the gift of the great beasts extended the people's food supply and distracted the young braves from their burning desire to wreak havoc on perceived enemies. Yellow Jacket and I were side-by-side munching grass as we ambled along while our riders kept vigil.

"The early spring grass is plentiful, Yellow Jacket, and the slow pace allows us to eat our fill."

"It's a good thing, too! The mares with new foals and the those ready to give birth would have a difficult time keeping up otherwise."

"Little Wolf is restless," I observed. "I think he wants to be among the older braves, but Spotted Elk told him guarding the horse herd is the most important assignment a brave could have."

"I heard Standing Bear tell him much the same when Little Wolf complained to his brother."

"You know, Yellow Jacket, I think that having you and Standing Bear riding heard with us today has lifted Little Wolf's spirits."

June 1, 1877
Standing Bear and Little Wolf

"I can't believe that we have less than two weeks of freedom remaining, Standing Bear. The warriors are increasing their war games and selecting those who are the best sharpshooters to outfit with the latest rifles. You know that I can shoot better than most of those getting the new firearms."

"Your marksmanship is well known, but Father is correct when he tells you that our wealth and survival depends on our horses. Protecting the combined herd is of greater importance than parading around stirring up trouble. You may get a chance to prove your abilities all too soon, little brother."

June 12, 1877
Spotted Elk and Songbird

Songbird approached her father as he prepared to mount his stallion. White Cloud seemed restless, and the slow progress was wearing on his war steed as much as it appeared to be on the young warriors of the combined bands.

"Father, may I have a word with you?"

"Mount your mare, and ride with me to the council meeting on the far side of the encampment. Joseph has called a meeting of the other chiefs and elders."

"I'm not surprised to hear this," Songbird said with a heavy heart. "It's become common knowledge that my murdered husband's brother, Whalitis, and two of his friends have disappeared from the camp overnight. Everyone in Chief Joseph's band knows that Whalitis swore revenge on the killer of Wind Blowing."

"It looks like this exodus from our homeland to avoid war will be a failed attempt, my daughter, and war will find us despite our efforts to avoid it." Spotted Elk shook his head sadly. "I estimate that we are only three days from the reservation. If those young hotheads kill anyone, we will all pay the price."

"Father, that is the reason for my request to return to your teepee. If the worst is to come, I would like to be with you, my mother, grandmother, and my brothers when I make my final journey. Also, I can be of help to mother and grandmother."

"Move your things to our camp, Daughter, you are welcome in my house. I'm sure Wind Song will welcome the help. Speckled Bird is fading from this world. My mother's body has become as frail as the bird for which she was named."

June 14, 1877

The people were up before dawn loading the travois and pack animals. The usually organized process appeared almost frantic. Little Wolf and I were still on night herd when Standing Bear and Yellow Jacket joined us. I listened and tried to understand the meaning of their words.

"Whalitis and his two companions have killed several settlers, Little Wolf. They waited a full day to get the murderer of Wind Blowing. They were unable to find the killer of his brother, so the trio killed another known hater of our people. Unfortunately, they also killed a couple of other innocent settlers who tried to intervene to save their friend."

"Is what I heard yesterday afternoon true? The talk then was that at least a half dozen warriors left camp to join them."

"Yes, brother, and they are raiding the homesteads on our ancestral lands. Joseph and Looking Glass have decided to make a break for it to join our old friends, the Crow, before the white man's soldiers can take revenge on our people."

Yellow Jacket thought that sounded like a solid plan, but I had a bad feeling about it. We headed east to the plains where our old hunting partners lived.

"We are moving too quickly for the young foals to keep up," Yellow Jacket pointed out.

I nodded my head in agreement. "They tire climbing these mountains, and I sense danger." I'd no more than made that comment to my friend when Little Wolf wheeled me around, and we took off at a full gallop toward the back of the herd. His rifle blazed away as he sent four wolves to the Happy Hunting Grounds. The pack of the predators had zeroed in on a newborn filly and her mother. The surviving wolves took flight when their four companions hit the ground.

Little Wolf reloaded his rifle, and dismounted to place the small terrified foal across my withers before he sprung up on my back behind the trembling infant. Her mother limped along beside me; she'd been injured trying to protect her baby.

The people made camp in the foothills of the Rocky Mountains to rest before the long climb upwards. The small filly was up on its shaky legs and nursing from its mother whose wounds had been tended.

Scouts were sent out and guards were posted at regular intervals. Standing Bear and two braves I did not know returned with a tall white man, a woman who looked like one of our people, and a small boy, not much older than Little Wolf had been when he 'd declared that I was his. The whole family wore buckskins and blanket-like jackets to ward off the chill of the approaching night.

As usual, Little Wolf and I were at our post guarding our charges well before dawn. Soon Standing Bear joined us. The people were ready to make the climb by first light. I listened to the conversation between the brothers.

"*Standing Bear, do you think the mountain man can be trusted?*"

"*Father said that he was an old friend of Joseph's, but I don't trust any white man.*"

"*At least the food stores he traded for the six mares with the youngest foals will see us across the mountains.*"

Those six mares and their young foals were the lucky ones. We lost many of our young foals to the hazardous mountain terrain and occasional attacks by the cougars that made their home in the rugged peaks. I sensed a great relief among many of our people when we crossed into the land of the Crow where the elders hoped to find shelter among their old friends.

Emissaries were sent to the Crow Chiefs. As a result the scouts and guards saw no danger when their old friends approached our encampment. But the Crow warriors surprised us. They swooped down to attack our people and steal many of our horses before we could drive them off.

At a full gallop once more on the plains where I'd hunted buffalo, I now hunted our friends turned enemies. Little Wolf was deadly with his rifle, but we were able to recover very few of the stolen members of our herd. The braves that were mounted during the attack reluctantly called a halt to the pursuit of the villainous raiders. Every warrior would be needed to protect the women, children, and old people, as well as the remainder of us horses.

Standing Bear and Little Wolf

"The chiefs have decided that the last chance for our people to live free is to flee to Canada where we may find a home like the Lakota. Sitting Bull has crossed the border and is now residing in the north where the Native People of this land are welcomed."

"Why are the soldiers stalking us, Standing Bear?" Little Wolf railed. "They force us off of our land with threats of war, and now they hunt us down to keep us from leaving the land they now claim as their own."

"I wish I could answer that, my brother. Unfortunately, the white man's thought process is so foreign that even our father can't understand it. He says their hearts are filled with hate for those who are different. But I think they are consumed with greed, and have no regard for Mother Earth, or the other life forms that share this land."

"Grandmother is becoming weaker. Even reclining on the travois is too much for her, and we can't slow down with the soldiers in pursuit."

August
Nightstalker

The white soldiers are relentless, but our war chiefs continue to evade them. Warriors comprise less than one third of our people's population, and they are fighting a vastly superior number of the enemy. Our guard precautions and several successful skirmishes have managed to buy our people time. We're cut off from the direct route to Canada, and are once more headed west into the mountains.

Time and again Little Wolf and I, along with other horse wranglers, pulled floundering foals from treacherous river crossings. The young and the old are becoming weaker with every day. We are moving too fast for them to keep up.

I talked with Yellow Jacket on a brief rest. "I missed you today on our travels, my friend."

"Standing Bear and I are riding rear guard. We spent hours looking for sneak attacks from the soldiers chasing us, and watching for warriors returning from skirmishes with the enemy."

"With every battle, my friend, the number of our warriors and warhorses diminishes a little more."

"I heard one of the advanced scouts tell Standing Bear that the soldiers were carving up our fallen steeds and cooking them for their dinner."

"Eww, yuck! How disgusting! What do they think we are—cattle or buffalo?"

"I know, Nightstalker, it gave me the creeps when I heard it."

"Yeah, me too! My skin just got all prickly. It is hard to imagine people eating horses."

A few days later, Little Wolf's grandmother, Speckled Bird, spread her wings for the trip to the afterworld. There was hardly time to celebrate her life and see her off on her last journey. Less than seven suns later, Little Wolf and I were assigned to the rear guard duties that had been Standing Bear and Yellow Jacket's post for the past several weeks. Standing Bear had just joined the band of warriors fighting the fierce hit-and run-battles with the blue coats. I sure hope the Great Spirit watches over them, and that Yellow Jacket doesn't end up as horse steaks!

Little Wolf and I were just taking up our position as rear guard when my ears pricked at an unfamiliar sound; he heard it too. He urged me slowly forward until we saw them. It was not quite dawn so they didn't see my dark coated form, nor did they spot Little Wolf wrapped in a buffalo hide to ward off the chill of the early morning fog. We walked softly until we were safely out of rifle range, then we hightailed it back to camp to raise the alarm.

Little Wolf gave the report to his father, the only person he was sure would take immediate action.

"Father, I saw soldiers near us and across the valley. As best as I can tell there are hundreds of them, all on foot, and sneaking up on our camp!"

"I will alert the chiefs and warriors in camp. We will speed up the move. Go back and help protect the horse herd, son. Get them moving, we can't afford to lose any more of them. They are our people's lifeline."

I picked up on the urgency in the voices of Little Wolf and his father. I responded to Little Wolf's request for speed, and charged forward like the great shadow warrior he thought I was.

It was a narrow escape for all of us. Our camp had nearly been surprised and overrun by the enemy.

The best two sharpshooters positioned themselves at the head of the canyon to give the families a chance to distance themselves from the persistent soldiers.

September 1877
Standing Bear on the battle at Canyon Creek

I wondered if other braves had to give accountings of battle, or did this dubious honor just fall on me because my father is a tribal elder?

"We fought the soldiers in a running battle from mid-morning until dark. We made good use of the sharpshooters among us to inflict damage on the enemy and slow them down."

"Were our warriors able to slow them as planned?" Chief Joseph inquired.

I tried to be respectful, but it was difficult. Chief Looking Glass appeared subdued. He had not been the same after suggesting the move to join up with the Crow that ended so badly. "We may have delayed them some, but we lost many great warhorses. It will be difficult to continue without them. The enemy was unnerved by the accurate fire of our mounted warriors who hung from the sides of their horses firing from a position beneath their necks."

"Did they retreat?" Spotted Elk asked. My father already knew the answer, but wanted the rest of them to hear it.

I took a deep breath and eased into the rest of my report. "No, the soldiers didn't back off. They tried driving us toward the rest of our people fleeing up Canyon Creek to the mouth of the canyon. Our sharpshooters stationed high above them behind tall boulders kept them at bay until dark. The ranking soldier made the mistake of dismounting his troops when falling under our sniper fire, or they may have succeeded in destroying us. They broke off at nightfall, unable to see us, but they will be back at daylight."

Then Joseph spoke, "Spotted Elk give the order to move camp before dawn."

Nightstalker
10 days later September 23, 1877

After our surprising victory at Canyon Creek that was largely due to Little Wolf spreading the alarm, we were moving even faster now. We headed north to the joining of the rivers called *Mussel Shell* and *Missouri*. We'd fought fierce battles with the Crow and Cheyenne scouts who worked for the soldiers chasing us.

I was worried about my friends, Yellow Jacket and Hopper, as well as their human riders. While Little Wolf and I patrolled the back of the herd; Spotted Elk lead a party of warriors on a raid for much needed supplies. I was even somewhat concerned about White Cloud, too, I guess. After all, he was carrying Spotted Elk.

Before they left for the supply raid, I overheard Little Wolf's father tell him that the army, and other white invaders, had supplies stored at the *Cow Island* crossing of the river called *Missouri.*

The raid was successful and the supplies helped to feed our hungry children. The children and the old people suffered the most on our forced flight to the north. It was that way with us horses, too. The long circuitous trail behind us included a multitude of water crossings that were littered with fallen foals, wounded steeds, and the old.

September 29, 1877
Spotted Elk

I woke in a cold sweat. "Wind Song!" She was startled by the fear in my voice. "Wake our daughter and sons. Pack lightly, only what you can carry astride Starlight, bring warm clothing for life in the mountains."

"Where are you going, husband?"

"I go to warn the chiefs."

They wouldn't heed my warning, and shrugged off my premonition. In my unsettling dream, I'd seen Snake Creek running red from a battle to begin in the coming days. My priorities shifted, now I must save my family.

Everyone was accounted for and ready to travel except my youngest son. "Standing Bear, find your brother and bring him back."

Nightstalker

Little Wolf and I were out early scouting the perimeter of the herd as had been our custom for many days, ever since the attempted sneak attack by foot soldiers. Things looked quiet. Where were the scouts and soldiers that had been dogging our trail? It had been two suns since we last saw them.

Yellow Jacket's golden coat and spotted white blanket brightened the predawn of the early morning. Standing Bear rode up close to us and whispered to his brother.

"Father wants you back at the lodge, now!"

Little Wolf didn't say a word; he just guided me to follow Yellow Jacket and his brother back to our temporary camp.

At the lodge I waited with Yellow Jacket while the sons conferred in quiet tones with their father.

This wasn't normal behavior, and I turned my head toward my friend. "Yellow Jacket, do you know what's happening?"

"I think we're leaving camp."

"I was thinking the same, but Wind Song is mounted on my mother! Usually Little Wolf's mother leads Starlight, like the other women whose horses pulled loaded travois."

"It's strange alright. The teepee is still standing, and next to nothing is packed."

Yellow Jacket was correct; Songbird was mounted on my grown-up little sister. She looked much the same as she did when I found her lost and crying as a foal. Songbird called her Moonbeam.

Hopper and Sundown joined us as we left camp. Sundown's elderly parents had been among the earliest casualties of this exodus. Best friends since childhood, Standing Bear and his parents were Sundown's second family.

Spotted Elk took up the lead once we hit the trail north. Wind Song followed on Starlight, her daughter riding Moonbeam close behind, and yours truly at rear guard with Little Wolf. His brother and Sundown were riding ahead acting as scouts for our small party.

October 2, 1877

So far we'd avoided the blue cavalry coming from the north. What the heck! I thought the blue coats were way behind us; days behind even the big camp and the horse herd that we'd left three suns back.

It was cold, but no campfires had been built since our small family group headed out on our own. My ears pricked and Little Wolf tensed when we heard loud cracks that meant rifle fire. It was coming from behind us. Spotted Elk put White Cloud in a flight across the ground, closely followed by his wife and daughter.

Little Wolf dropped me back so that we could fight and give our family a chance to escape. We were badly out numbered, but Little Wolf let out a fierce war cry and we charged, closing the distance between ourselves, and the advancing group of soldiers. Little Wolf's rifle cracked in my ears. Ouch! I pinned my ears back tight along my neck. That helped muffle the loud report of the rifle; it also made me look mean and ferocious! I wrinkled up my nose and bared my teeth for the added intimidation factor.

Little Wolf had taken out three of the five blue clad enemies. Additional rifle fire reinforced Little Wolf's own when Yellow Jacket and Hopper joined me in the charge. Our three braves quickly dispatched the remaining soldiers.

Standing Bear ordered a retreat. "*Quickly, we need to catch up with the rest of our family. Sundown and I took on a couple of scouts north of here and were on our way back when we saw them take off on the run, and heard your war cry followed by rifle fire.*"

I picked up on the dire situation and gave Little Wolf the fastest ride of his life as I gobbled up the rocky terrain never missing a step. Yellow Jacket and Hopper were right along side of me. We'd almost caught up with the rest of our party that was nearing the northern part the water known as Snake Creek when more cavalry horses came up behind us.

Our riders slowed the three of us; we gulped fresh air into our lungs and rested briefly as we watched the galloping riders approach, and listened to our riders' conversation.

"*Where did they come from, brother?*"

"The soldiers that you fought, Little Wolf, were either an advance party or part of a larger unit that got lost. The others must have spurred their horses when they heard the sounds of the battle."

"They sure look determined to catch us, brother."

Sundown commented on the condition of the advancing horses. *"They've run their horses into the ground trying to make up the distance between us."*

Standing Bear assessed their approach. *"Time to go! They're almost within rifle range, and some of them can shoot while riding."*

Darn! I think Standing Bear misjudged the range of the enemy's rifle fire. A pain tore through my hip, and I tumbled to the rocky ground. Little Wolf, fortunately, fell free of me. He stood, and I was relieved to know that he was unharmed.

Standing Bear and my old friend, Yellow Jacket, returned to save Little Wolf. His brother pulled him up behind him. The last I saw of my friends they were headed north at a full gallop. Little Wolf looked back and called to me. "*Get up Nightstalker! Get up and follow us!*

Then, I heard a chilling war cry from Sundown! He was making a charge on the two mounted soldiers who'd halted to take better aim at our retreating backs when their spent mounts could no longer keep up with us.

I staggered to my feet in time to see Sundown dispatch two riflemen. Another soldier was fast closing in on him! The mounted soldier was so focused on Sundown and Hopper that I doubt he even noticed me. I took a deep breath and launched my body at the oncoming enemy.

I hit horse and rider broadside! The cavalry horse and I crashed to the ground in a tangle of thrashing legs. The other horse headed south when we were both able to gain our feet, and he left his rider moaning on the battlefield trying to get his bearings.

Sundown let out another war cry, then wheeled Hopper around to head north "*Follow me Nightstalker!*" He yelled back at me.

I was panting hard now. The scrapes and bruises from my two collisions with the ground, not to mention the cuts from the darn metal shoes of the other horse, were painful. But I was more concerned with the feeling of blood gushing from my wounded hip. I gathered what strength I could and followed Hopper.

Soldiers were still chasing us from behind when we ran smack into another group coming from the north. "OH! HORSE POOP! We'e cut off!"

Sundown turned sharply east toward the cliff like bank above the river. At a full gallop, Hopper jumped into the red tinged water below. I jumped right behind them. A sharp pain cut across my back just below my withers. We dove beneath the surface, but the bullets followed us making a strange buzz as they ripped through the water. It sounded like angry hornets whizzing past us.

I resurfaced to find Hopper far ahead of me, but I didn't see Sundown. Swimming was becoming difficult, and I went under again. When I reached the surface once more, my heart broke. I tried to swim with the current, but I got tangled up with the bodies of other horses. Some of them were only weanlings and yearlings. Like the hapless buffalo herd killed by the white invaders from the fowl smelling train on the plains; we were being eliminated! Soldiers had killed anyone with a spotted coat pattern that could be easily identified as belonging to the Nez Perce.

My strength was fading as I went under for the third time. I held my breath and fought for my life!

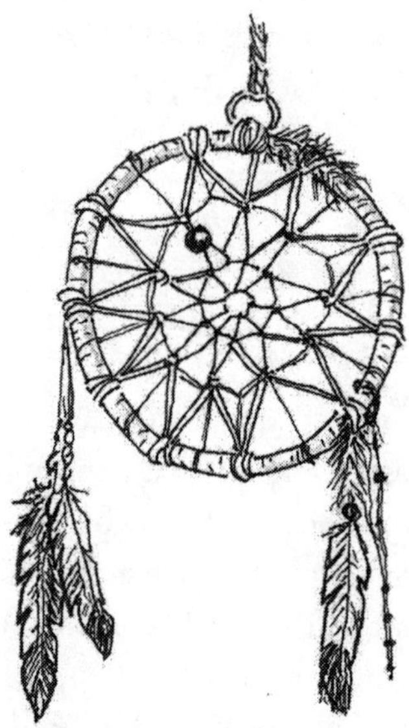

9

On the other side

"Oh no!" I whinnied a second time as I sunk into a bottomless black void. The last thing I heard was Marcie screaming, ""*Frosty!*" *as* icy water snuck into my nostrils, and I fought panic. The thought occurred to me that I'd been in this situation before, and this was my second chance at life. I didn't want to drown; I held my breath as I made one more huge effort to lurch to the surface. A bright light—the sun I think—beckoned to me. If I could just reach it I would be safe and able to breathe fresh air again. Once more, I had an odd sense that I'd been down in this cold deep water for a hundred years! And in that moment, I felt a tug on my head, and pressure around my heart-girth; something was pulling me upward. That was all the help I needed to break the strange hold the dark water had on me.

I scrambled out of the water scraping my legs on the shale. Water came out of my nose when I snorted. I looked around, totally disorientated. Then, I recognized Marcie who was as soaked as me!

George rode Joker up close to me, and he removed a lariat from my saddle horn. That must have been the tug that I felt when my saddle girth tightened around my middle; Marcie still had a death grip on my reins that she'd used to yank my head above the water.

She was crying and hugging me now, but I blew water all over her trying to clear it from my lungs and nostrils.

"*What the heck happened, Marcie?*" George cried out.

That's what I wanted to know too. What the heck happened?

"I don't know, George. We were following you across the river when Frosty just sunk beneath me. It was like the river was trying to swallow us."

Horse Pucky!!! Hadn't I been trying to clue her in for years that rivers were dangerous?

"*Are you okay, Marcie?*" George wrapped his arms around her tightly.

"I'm fine, George. Thanks to you and your habit of carrying a rope on our trail rides, I was able to get a loop around the horn."

Marcie, the rope I threw was to pull you out. I didn't expect even you to dive back in that freezing water to attach it to the saddle!"

Oh! Well…thank you, honey," She kissed him on the cheek. *"I want Doc Wiley to look at Frosty. He's kind of banged up, not to mention all the cold water he inhaled."*

"We can call him from Mom and Dad's place when we pick up the kids. It's closer than home anyway."

Doc Wiley checked me over and the crazy guy tried to drown me again! He stuck a tube up my nostril; I swallowed as it snaked its way to my stomach. To my total shock he poured a large bottle of what Marcie called *"mineral oil"* into a funnel attached to the offensive tube. Then he gave me a tetanus booster, an antibiotic shot to combat infection, and he gave Marcie a jar of more antibiotic in a powder form.

He instructed her, "*Sprinkle this on his feed once a day until it is gone. And, Marcie, keep him out of the water until next summer. His immune system may be compromised for a while.*"

When I heard that, I instantly forgave him for the painful removal of small rocks and debris from the cuts on my legs, all the needles he stuck me with, and the gross tube invasion.

No more river crossings? YAHOOO! At-a way to go, Doc!

George and Marcie October 3, 1977

"*I got a call back this afternoon from the park service, George.*"

"*What did they say?*"

"*They removed the fallen tree, and declared the crossing was in excellent condition. They reported there was not a place in the river anywhere close by that was deep enough to submerge a horse. I packed the kids in the car, dropped them off with your parents, and drove over there. You know, just to make sure they were at the correct river crossing.*

Several park rangers and maintenance people were down at the bottom of Little Cedar Point Hill checking both of the crossings. I showed them the spot where I almost lost Frosty yesterday."

"*And did they locate the hole?*"

"*No! They walked it, and then I walked it, too. The rocky bed of the river bottom was solid, footing was okay, and the depth of the water only rose just few inches above my knees!*"

"*What the heck happened then, Marcie? I was there and saw the two of you disappear from sight.*"

"*It beats me, George. It's next to impossible for a sinkhole to refill so quickly. But I wonder if Frosty's fear of the water all these years was some kind of premonition of yesterday's near miss with disaster?*"

"*Too bad we can't ask him, Marcie.*"

"*Maybe Ken at Hi-Low was right, years ago, when he said Frosty was an old soul. What if Frosty did have a past life, and what happened yesterday had some bizarre connection with it?*"

George winced. "Please, Marcie, tell me that you don't really believe in all that stuff!"

"Okay, explain how else the strange whirlpool cropping up, after you and Joker had just safely traveled the same path, could even be possible, George?"

"I can't explain it, Marcie." He tossed up his hands in bewilderment.

"EXACTLY!"

10

Canada
Mid November 1877

Standing Bear and Spotted Elk

"*I'm worried about your brother, Standing Bear.*" Spotted Elk frowned. "*He hasn't eaten much, and he spends too much time looking to the south.*"

"*I know, Father, Little Wolf still hopes that Nightstalker will join us, as did Sundown and Hopper.*"

"*I doubt that. He would be here by now, if at all able. It would have been better when Sundown told his tale, if he'd simply said that Nightstalker was now with The Great Spirit. Your mother is terrified that Little Wolf will try to go find his horse.*"

"*My brother is no longer an impulsive child, Father. He's a warrior tested in battle. I don't think Mother needs to worry that he would do something so foolish.*"

Little Wolf

Hunting without Nightstalker seems strange to me. My sister lent me her mare, Moonbeam, for the hunt. Songbird and Standing Bear told me the story of how Nightstalker had rescued his little sister not long before he saved me. I stroked the mare's white spotted neck as I thought of the bravery of my great shadow warrior.

"What are you thinking, brother? You seem far away." *Standing Bear said, putting a hand on my shoulder."*

"I was thinking that both Moonbeam and I would already be in the after-life if not for the bravery of Nightstalker."

"So would Sundown. He said that Nightstalker saved him by charging a cavalry horse when its rider was taking aim at him as he battled two other soldiers."

"Yes, he told me. He said that Nightstalker followed him and Hopper north where they were cut off. They all jumped into the river, and that was the last time that Sundown saw him. He told me that my brave warhorse was badly wounded."

"Well... Little Wolf, maybe like Sundown and Hopper he was able to escape the river, and will show up when we least expect it?"

He's gone, brother, I can feel his loss," I closed my fist on my chest, *"deep where my heart beats. I pray to The Great Spirit that his bravery merits another chance at life."*

"We all pray for that little brother. Nightstalker was a member of our family for many years." Standing Bear did his best to change my line of thought. *"But, now we need to concentrate our efforts on the hunt if our family is to survive the long winter.*

I rode Moonbeam on many hunts that winter providing food for our family. About fifty warriors had joined us in exile. They were all that managed to evade being forced onto reservations. They added to the hunts, as well as providing extra protection for the handful of families, including ours who now lived in our little village.

In the spring of 1878 Sundown and Songbird became husband and wife. Sundown moved out of the bachelor tepee that he had been sharing with Standing Bear and me. That summer I painted some of Nightstalker's greatest exploits on the outside of our lodge.

My brother helped by suggesting ideas from hunts where he or my father rode our brave horse. Standing Bear and Songbird decided to mate Yellow Jacket to Moonbeam, and I was to have the foal.

I'm not sure how I feel about that, but I am humbled by their generosity and love.

April 1879

Though in a strange land, we are still free, and I'm now an uncle!

"Your daughter is beautiful, sister. I carved a small horse as a gift for my new niece. "Thank you, Little Wolf. I will keep it for her until she is old enough to appreciate it."

Four weeks later Standing Bear hauled me out of our lodge as the rising sun was just peeking over the snowcapped mountains. "*Hurry, brother, your new horse is about to be born!*"

Moonbeam had foaled. The black colt with a large white hip blanket that was loaded with spots lurched to his feet at our approach. He scampered to his mother's side and pressed himself against her larger body, but he didn't nurse. Like a dark shadow against Moonbeam's side, he flattened his ears and tried to focus on what he perceived as a threat.

Standing Bear laughed. "*He's already prepared to take on what he thinks may be an enemy. I think you will have your hands full with this one, little brother!*"

Right then and there, I decided to call him Shadow. Once more I prayed to The Great Spirit. "*Great Father, let my shadow warrior, Nightstalker, find a home in a peaceful land where he is honored and valued. Please let him find friendship, and become a member of a loving family.*"

End

APPENDIX

PARTS OF A HORSE
Illustrated by Jackie Anton

1. Muzzle
2. Nostril
3. Cheek
4. Face
5. Eye
6. Forelock
7. Ear
8. Mane
9. Neck
10. Throatlatch
11. Withers
12. Back
13. Loin
14. Croup
15. Hip
16. Tail
17. Point of Buttocks
18. Stifle
19. Flank
20. Gaskin
21. Hock
22. Hoof or Foot
23. Pastern
24. Fetlock
25. Cannon bone
26. Knee
27. Forearm
28. Shoulder
29. Sock
30. Stocking

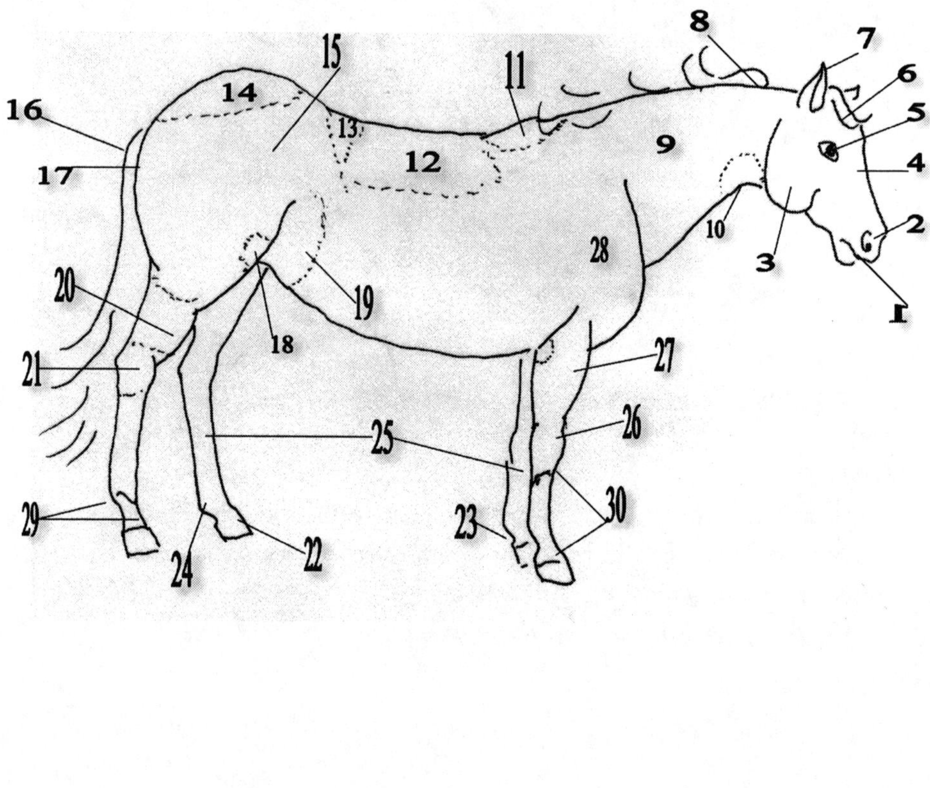

VOCABULARY

Bay - Any shade of brown horse with black main, tail, and black points. Points are the tips of the ears, the muzzle, and black on the legs from the knees and hocks down.

Buckskin - A golden-colored horse with the same black markings and points as a bay horse.

Colt- A male horse under four years of age.

Counting coup - refers to the winning of prestige in battle, rather than having to prove a win by injuring one's opponent. Warriors won prestige by acts of bravery in the face of the enemy, and these acts could be recorded in various ways and retold as stories. Any blow struck against the enemy counted as a coup, but the most prestigious acts included touching an enemy warrior with the hand, bow, or with a coup stick then escaping unharmed. Touching the first enemy to die in battle or touching the enemy's defensive works also counted as coup. Counting coup could also involve stealing an enemy's weapons or horses tied up to his lodge in camp. Risk of injury or death was required to count coup. Escaping unharmed while counting coup was considered a higher honor than being wounded in the attempt.

Déjà - vu -is a word of French origin that literally means, ***"already seen."*** It is the phenomenon of having the strong sensation that an event or experience currently being experienced has been experienced in the past

Filly - A female horse under four years of age.

Foal - A baby horse.

Gelding - A male horse that has been neutered.

Hand - A hand is four inches. It is the measurement for a horse, taken from the ground to the point of the withers. Example a fifteen hand horse would be equal to 60 inches. A fifteen-two hand horse would equal sixty-two inches.

Larder - A stored supply of food, especially for winter.

Long-line or Lunge line - Is a long lead that is usually fifteen to twenty feet long with a snap at one end.

Mare - A female horse four years of age or older.

1 Moon = 1 month.

Palomino - A golden-colored horse with white or cream manes and tails. May have one or more white markings on their legs.

Parti-Colored Skin - A term used by Appaloosa owners to describe the pink and black mottled skin on their horses.

Seven suns is the same as seven days or one week.

Stallion - A male horse four years of age or older that is usually kept for breeding.

Suckling - A young animal that is still feeding on its mother's milk.

Travois - a sled made of two poles connected by a frame and pulled by an animal, used in the past by Native North American Peoples.

Weanling - A young horse that has just been taken off its mother's milk.

Yearling - A horse between one and two years old. The term yearling also applies to calves and deer of the same age.

REFERENCES

Nez Perce website. http://nezperce.org/Official/mainpages/resources.htm University of Idaho Extension District 1 Nez Perce Reservation

http://www.friendsnezpercebattlefields.org/7th-cavalry-in-the-nez-perce-war.htm Historical Review written for the 125th Anniversary of the Battle at Big Hole by John Doerner from a paper delivered October 2002 at The Big Hole National Battlefield.

http://www.historynet.com/nez-perce-war.htm Nez Perce War / History Net

http://www.pbs.org/weta/thewest/people/a_c/chiefjoseph.htm PBS People New Perspectives on THE WEST " Chief Joseph" Hin-mah-too-yah-lat-kekt (1840 - 1904)

http://www.users.globalnet.co.uk/~chrisson/apphist3.htm

MEET THE AUTHOR

Jackie Anton is the author of **"Backyard Horse Tales: Sox 2nd Edition"** winner of the prestigious Mom's Choice Award Silver Seal of Excellence.

An accomplished equestrian with a lifetime of experience working with horses and children, the author has brought an insight and empathy for both to her Backyard Horse Tales.

Frosty and the Nightstalker is a trip back in time, where Sox's tale is of a modern day horse. Each presents an enlightening trip in to the minds and adventures of two very different horses.

BYHT 3: Don't Call Me Love is in the works. The first four chapters of Love's tale was released as "Prelude: Backyard Horse Tales 3: Don't Call Me Love" March of 2012 to excellent reviews. The preview to Love's adventures is available as an e-book on Smashwords.com Amazon kindle, and other e-reader points of purchase.

Author Contacts
Book Web Site: www.backyardhorsetales.com
Author Web Site: http://talesbyjackie.com
Blog: http://jackieanton.com/

ILLUSTRATOR

Sandy Shipley

Sandy Shipley was born a "horsey" kid. As soon as she could hold a pencil she began drawing horses. She got her beloved Rex, her first horse at age 14. She began art lessons at the same age and attended Cooper School of Art after high school graduation.

As an adult she became a commercial artist and text book illustrator, jobs that afforded funds for her to own, train, and show horses as well as teaching horsemanship and riding. She merged her two great loves, horses and art by doing portraits of beloved equines, canines, and an occasional human. Her knowledge of anatomy and love of nature, as reflected in her artwork, have been useful tools.

Today, Sandy works at Valley Tack Shop as a buyer, saddle fitter, and artist. She lives in Northeastern Ohio where she shares her home with her French Bulldog, Maggie, a cat named, Fred, and two box turtles. She is also a proud mom, mother-in-law, and grandmother.

Sandy wishes to thank Jackie Anton for the opportunity to illustrate "Frosty and the Nightstalker." Sandy says, "This is the realization of a lifelong dream, to illustrate a story written for youngsters."

E-mail: ***ship1941@sbcglobal.net***

"DON'T CALL ME LOVE"

An Excerpt from Backyard Horse Tales 3

I was turned out alone in a small paddock on my second day. Lou groomed me in the morning and talked to me, but I only understood a few words. *"You can spend most of the day in the riding arena, Love. You will be close to the other horses, but separated until you get acquainted with them."*

I watched the four older horses from the safety of my isolated turnout area. The riding arena at my new home was a far cry from the huge pastures where I had spent the first year of my life. The only grass was at the edges of the fence lines. The adults ran around the larger paddock bucking, rearing, and playing tag. I raised my tail so high that it curled over my back, snorted, shook my head, and whizzed around my playpen.

It didn't take long for the other horses to calm down. That's just how it is with older horses, I guess. Soon the adult residents of this little farm were busy munching grass. I walked slowly around my pen behind the barn eating the sparse grass at the edges when the approach of two horses distracted me from my pursuit of tasty green morsels. A patch of clover had sidetracked one of the advancing horses, both were mares, and the tall black one with a high head carriage leaned over the fence.

"Hello," she said. She sounded friendly, so I wandered over to talk with her. As I approached, she introduced herself.

"My name is Kid-O. What's your name?"

I moved closer and cautiously touched noses with her as I answered her question. "I am called *Love.*" Kid-O didn't know me yet, so she was unable to comment on the irony of my name.

She just laughed and said, "Humans sure pick funny names for us. My first owner was a doctor, and he named me *Caduceus Heather*, but my new owner hated it. He called me *Kid-O* because I was the youngest when I first came here."

Intrigued, I asked her, "How old were you?"

"I was about your age, I guess. It was just past my first birthday when I arrived. That was three years ago, by the human's calendar."

"And you are the youngest?" I thought the others must be really old!

"Yep, and as the only *Morgan* I am outnumbered by *stock horses.*"

"What's a stock horse?" That was a new term for me.

Kid-O laughed and looked over her shoulder at the others. "You and everyone else here have ranch horses in your heritage, and will most likely be Western horses."

We paused in our conversation to watch the approach of a blood bay mare with a huge white blanket decorated with a zillion bay haloed spots. She had no face markings or white on her black legs. Her black mane and tail ruffled in the mild breeze.

Kid-O introduced us. "Millie, this is Love the newest member of our herd."

The pretty bay Appaloosa mare looked me over, then touched noses with me. "Do you have a registered name, Love?"

"My mother told me that my registered name was Chelsea Love." I said this kind of disgusted, like I hated my name. The bay mare picked up on my attitude in a flash.

"Well, it could be worse. Just look at the name Kid-O has to show under. My registered name is Chilly Millie, and I get more than my share of bad jokes about it from the boys in our group."

Both mares moved over a little to make room for a dapple-gray gelding who had been close enough to overhear the conversation we girls were having. He was bigger than Millie who was not much taller than me, but twice my width. Kid-O still had a couple of inches on him at the withers although she appeared much taller due to her high headset.

He looked me over much the same way Millie had; the difference was the devilish look in his eyes. I had absolutely zero experience with grown male horses, but I remembered how rough the colts were before we were separated as yearlings.

"Hello, little Spots, I'm Cutter. You're sure a pretty little filly. When do you suppose you will be able to come out and keep us company?"

I wasn't sure if he was trying to be friendly, or just to testing my temper. But I set him straight. "My name isn't 'Spots,' it is Chelsea Love! While I don't really like my name, it beats the heck out of being called Spots." I laid my ears back and snorted at him for emphasis.

Cutter just laughed at my display of temper. He then told me something that I would remember for the rest of my life. "My name isn't really Cutter. It's the name my first owner gave me after our first season of Cutting Horse competitions. He told me, '*You've earned a better name than Squeaky.*'"

That was a bit of a shock, and I tried not to laugh. This large muscular guy with a resonant masculine voice couldn't have such a silly name, so I asked for clarification on the name change and the cutting thing. "What is a *cutting horse?*"

"A cutting horse works with cattle, moving them from one place to another. Sometimes we have to separate cows, calves, or steers from the herd to be branded or doctored. However, in competitions we 're judged on how quietly we go into the herd, separate the calf our rider selects, and our ability to keep that critter from returning to the herd. We can work up to three in the time allotted."

I really didn't know much more than before I'd asked him. It might have made more sense if I had a clue what a cow was, but I did not want to appear ignorant; so I just nodded my head, like I knew exactly what he was telling me.

"Someday, you may be able to earn a name you like better than Love. See y'all later, bye little one." He turned away to join a larger dark horse in the pasture.

Millie whispered to me, "I told you your name could be worse. As a baby, Cutter was named *Big Boys Squeaky Toy.*"

The three of us giggled at the strange name that had been given to him as a young foal. When the others wandered back to their grazing I decided that Chelsea Love wasn't so bad after all. Still, a cool nickname would be super.

The following day went much like the one before, except I had to splay my legs wide while turning my head to the side and stretching my neck to reach the taller grass on the other side of my fenced in enclosure. My three new friends stopped by in the afternoon to say hello and chat.

Then they abruptly turned away to make room for the huge dark horse. I had seen this behavior before, like my mother in the broodmare band—this was the boss horse. He was as tall as Kid-O, but twice as wide as the slim mare. Muscles bulged under his dark coat, and a white star sat dead center of his forehead. His pink muzzle looked like a child had splattered black paint on it with a watercolor brush. He was a dark chocolate color with black spots scattered on his coat. The only white on him other than his head was a small sock on one hind leg, and snowflakes across his rump. His mane and tail were black.

His size and strength was intimidating, but his eyes were kind. I was expecting him to sound like Cutter with a strong male voice, but his was much deeper, like the rumble of thunder, when he spoke.

"The others tell me that you're Chelsea Love. Is that correct?"

I heard my mother's voice in my head, *"Don't let anyone push you around, daughter."* I tried to draw on the strength she had instilled in me before I answered him.

"Yeah, that's the name I was given. What of it?" Okay, that came out a little bratty and hostile. But he didn't seem to take any offence with my attitude. However, he looked at me like I was a bug that he could squash whenever he chose. He picked up the questioning again.

"Do you know your father's name?"

"My mother told me my sire's name is Chief Chelsea." I tried to be a little more polite this time.

"Well then, it looks like you are my little sister. Chelsea is also my sire."

Sometimes the devil gets the better of me. I responded belligerently. "No. That only makes us a *half* brother and sister. I'm sure you are much older than my mother."

He gave me that insignificant bug look again, turned his big butt on me, and walked away without another word.

"Hey, old guy! What's your name?" I yelled after him.

He turned just long enough to grace me with a response. "They call me Frosty."

CPSIA information can be obtained at www.ICGtesting.com
Printed in the USA
LVOW132054290413

331486LV00001B/9/P

9 781457 517518